# CHAMPLAIN STORIES

∞

## Dulcimer Hill

*mle nevin*

Ruyinn.com

***Champlain Stories ∞ Dulcimer Hill***
Copyright © 2017 by Ruyinn LLC
Published by Ruyinn LLC
Key logo copyright © 2013 by Ruyinn LLC
Cover and Layout copyright © 2017 by Ruyinn LLC
Cover photograph © Can Stock Photo Inc./narapornm
Cover photograph © Can Stock Photo Inc./xzgorik

*RuyinnLLC@gmail.com*

ISBN: 978-0-9973209-6-1

# mle nevin

## Champlain Stories

∞

Changing Course
Ever After
Dulcimer Hill
*FIRE*

# CHAMPLAIN STORIES

∞

*Dulcimer Hill*

# CHAPTER ONE

## Now ~ Year 1

At the end of the empty row of seats in the rear of the hall, a heavy man maneuvered himself into a folding wooden chair, a chair that now seemed fragile and small. Margaret Renfrew realized she was staring. She looked away, then glanced again in his direction. Two seats, actually.

She'd seen no one at all like him in the ten years she and her husband had been coming north to work at the summer music school. This man wore enormous denim overalls and a red plaid shirt. Unruly dark hair, a youngish face. In his thirties, she guessed. He shifted his bulk with difficulty.

Margaret turned her eyes to the front of the hall, where chairs, microphone, and piano were all in place on the stage, ready for this evening's concert. This one was the first student performance of the year. The youngest, the eleven-year-olds, would play simple short pieces tonight. This was their first opportunity to become comfortable with the audience. These youngest students were crucial to the music school's future. If their parents weren't satisfied, the school would have a short future, a matter of a few years at most.

She glanced again toward the enormous man at the end of the row. Really, she thought, he must be a joke.

1

Certainly some of the local people were what she'd call country bumpkins, if she wanted to be unkind, but this young man had deliberately dressed the part. And his size. How could anyone let himself go like that? She did not believe obesity was a disease. It was clearly a failure of character. She was a slender gray-haired woman who had kept herself trim through fifty-nine years.

Outside the performance shed, evening sun turned to twilight. The heat of a long July day lingered, curling in through the wide screened windows and rising through the open trusses until it met the pine-board roof. Margaret watched the audience from her seat in the last row of chairs. Families, students, and faculty moved uncomfortably in their seats. Wooden chairs with hard straight slats were a summer music school tradition.

Margaret wondered what had delayed the start of the season's first student recital. Behind her, the screen door at the back of the shed creaked open and then clattered shut, announcing another late arrival. She didn't turn to look but hoped the student ushers had not run out of programs. Her assistant in the school office had run off the supply this afternoon. She sighed. Whatever the backstage crisis holding things up, Henry, the school's jack-of-all-trades and Margaret's husband, would be coping.

Tomorrow was the Renfrews' day off. She would speak to Henry tonight about getting away, skipping their cabin chores, not worrying so much about the school's equipment. What was the point of summer near the beautiful western shore of Lake Champlain if you seldom got to gaze at mountains across the lake, savor the scents of woods and water and meadows, or enjoy nature's sonatas?

She looked again at the oversized young man and caught herself in her own assumption. Why did she think he was local? Because he looked it, she answered herself. He was an enormous pear-shaped caricature of a mountain man. But he might be here because of some student. No, Margaret thought. Impossible.

At the front of the wood-paneled hall, Kenneth Anderson, the school's new director, a balding man in a brown cashmere vest and tweed jacket despite the heat, chatted up a pair of well-dressed parents. Margaret noticed Dr. Anderson try to glance at his watch surreptitiously.

Kenneth Anderson was the reason Margaret so looked forward to her day off. This was his first season at the school. He had been brought in from a private academy in the south, and he was proving to be a difficult boss. For one thing, he was considerably younger than Margaret, but then, these days, who wasn't? For another, Dr. Anderson wished to make a difference, by which he meant, of course, impressing the Board. Not an easy thing to do, as the Board members had musical backgrounds, several quite distinguished, and Dr. Anderson did not. He'd been hired for his fundraising skills and to sort out the school's precarious financial position. Perhaps, Margaret thought, she could plant the idea of improved seating in the performance shed: comfortable, slightly cushioned chairs, a little wider, a little curved, designed for modern bodies. Something tangible to mark the start of Dr. Anderson's tenure. But the end of hers and Henry's, she feared.

Young Susanna Hemelin came in the door at the front of the hall and trudged to the back to sit beside Margaret. Margaret smiled at the glum face, offering the welcoming security she knew the child needed. Susanna should not be here at all. At thirteen, she was stocky and socially awkward. Like Margaret and Henry, and unlike the other teenagers here, Susanna was not a gifted musician. Susanna's younger half-brother, Jordan Kesto, had the musical talent. A very great deal of talent. Their mother worked as a cabin counselor to pay Jordan's tuition. Margaret looked at the chunky girl, with her curly dark hair and colorful mismatched clothes, rather more clothes than most girls her age were wearing these days, and smiled again. Susanna returned the smile wanly, and Margaret patted the child's knee.

Donald Jessup, a nice young man who'd been Dean of Faculty for the last three years, peered out of the door at the rear of the stage. He walked out, tapped the microphone, and cleared his throat. The backstage problem had been resolved. Kenneth Anderson looked openly at his watch. Margaret turned her attention to the students being introduced. The youthful players took their seats for the Mendelssohn quartet.

The next morning, entering her office in the music camp's administration building, Margaret stopped at the desk of Kellie Brent, her comfortable, reliable summer assistant. Kellie was one of the locals herself. She had lived nearby all of her thirty-six years. She was a fruitful source of information for faculty and staff who were here only during July and August – early June to the end of August in Margaret and Henry Renfrew's case.

During the winter, Margaret managed the office work from her home in Baltimore, and Henry, long retired from teaching college geography, puttered contentedly at home and as the summer school's equipment manager.

Margaret described the fat man at the end of the row at last night's concert. Kellie twisted a strand of her over-bleached hair as she listened to Margaret's description of the man who had taken up two seats.

"Oh, Lord," Kellie said. "That had to have been Will Ehrendorf." She made a face. "There was a time he wasn't like that. I wonder what he was doing here."

♫

## Then ~ Year 1

Julia Levan turned her head at the sound of footsteps on twigs and saw the fat little kid with the damp red face. He looked alarmed at the sight of her, as well he should. The hill where she sat, and its glorious view of the lake, belonged to her family.

The Ehrendorf boy, Julia knew. The brother of Sharon, her little sister Cathy's friend.

"D'you come up Rocky Knob a lot?" Julia asked from her cross-legged perch on the lichen-covered rock. She had always despised that name, Rocky Knob.

"Uh, sometimes," the boy replied. He stood at the edge of the trees. He was poised to turn and blunder back down the way he had come. He must have been to church or something, with the loosened tie and the sweaty wrinkled white dress shirt spilling out of navy slacks. His hair was dark brown and curling with damp.

The Ehrendorfs owned the farm adjacent to her family's land. According to Julia's grandmother, the Ehrendorfs were not the most neighborly of folks. According to her uncles and their cousins, that hardly mattered, as they weren't the sort of people one knew. An exception had been made for the Ehrendorfs' daughter, Sharon, when Cathy and she made friends during the summer reading program at the village library. And the mother, a school teacher, Mary Fran, was pleasant enough, they had to allow. It was the father, Walter Ehrendorf, a surly man who ignored property lines in hunting season and on snowmobile trails, who caused the aggravation.

And now the boy was trespassing. He seemed to know it. But Julia, too, would make an exception, for a child, for Cathy, whose friendship with Sharon had withered this year, to Cathy's bewilderment and distress.

"Hey, it's okay," she said now. "You can stay. Do you climb the hill sometimes, or sometimes you climb it a lot?"

"Last year." He was nervous, standing in the hot sun on a late August afternoon. "It's nice up here," the boy explained, "and it's neat how much of the lake you can see." He gestured out at the long narrow stretch of blue, a half mile away as a crow would fly. The hill they were on faced southeast on its open side. The boy said, "So this year I sneaked up here again."

"What is this, a special day?"

"It's my birthday," he said solemnly. His brown eyes and his damp brown curls were cute. She wondered what he'd look like if he ever grew out of the baby fat.

"Is it?" she said with a smile. "Happy birthday, Billy Ehrendorf. How old are you now?"

"Thirteen," the boy replied. "I'm a teenager now."

"Two years older than Sharon and Cathy, right? They don't seem to be friends any more."

"Sharon would," he said. "It's our dad. He doesn't want us playing with you. Think you're so much better'n us. You and the faggy eco-freaks, try to tell us how to live. He wants you all to go away. Or else," Billy added.

7

"I heard about it," Julia said. A barn had been set on fire and the windows of an office smashed. "My family was pretty mad themselves. Is that why you had to sneak up the hill?"

"Well, it's your property, not ours." With that admission, he scuffed the toe of his shoe on the brittle brown pine needles.

Julia nodded. "I tell you what, Billy Ehrendorf. It's okay to climb Rocky Knob yourself, as long as it's just on your birthday. But stay on the trail," she added. "If anyone asks, I said it's all right."

He had a cute grin.

♬

"Julie, dearest," Alice Fletcher said. "You mustn't think that it's your fault." Alice set her empty gin and tonic glass carefully on the wide arm of her chair.

Julia, slumped in another wooden chair, sat up and lifted her own drink. She noticed her chair's white paint beginning to peel. She shaded her eyes from the rays of the late afternoon sun angling off the steel rail between the piazza and the steep slope beyond, then turned her gaze toward her grandmother.

"Dad said it's a natural time to break up the family because I'm leaving for college." Julia paused. "I could stay home," she said to her grandmother. "I could go to school in New York."

"Your father, I'm afraid, is a cad."

That brought a smile to Julia's face. "And a bounder,

8

too, Grandmama?" she asked. "Are you going to say you always suspected?"

"No such thing ever crossed my mind," Alice said forthrightly. "But it's hurt your mother, discovering all the years of deception."

"I know," Julia said quietly. "I hate him for that. But only for that," she added.

"Yes, only that," her grandmother said. "I've got friends in what we used to call Boston marriages. Like your father, they should be allowed to live as they like. They should not have to live a lie."

"What's it for men? Philadelphia?"

"That's my girl," Alice said. "And without his lies, we wouldn't have you. Or Cathy. Elinor tries to remember that. Please don't burden her with guilt about what it's doing to you."

Julia stood and tossed her head to rearrange the fall of straight brown hair. She looked Alice in the eye. "I know what you're going to say, Grandmama. 'This too shall pass.' Would you like another G and T?"

♪

## Then ~ Year 2

"Hi," Billy Ehrendorf said. He watched Julia Levan climb the last few yards and sit down beside him on the expanse of rock in her T-shirt and jeans, just like a regular person. His sister Sharon had said that Julia was seven years older than Cathy. So she was nineteen. Billy glanced sideways at the slender young woman with long dark hair. He remembered the spooky feeling he'd had when he went in the CD store in the mall at Cumberland and there was this poster with her on it, her and her violin. Now that same famous person was here, up on the hill with him. He liked that. It wasn't the cool kind of thing he'd tell anybody about – she wasn't a rock star or anything – but he liked it.

"How come you don't get lost down there on that side?" he asked. Last fall, he'd tried to follow the path down toward where her family's houses were. He'd gotten lost. He'd kept going downhill, trying not to panic, until finally he came to the road that led back toward his own family's house.

"I did get lost once. Now I have a compass," Julia said. She touched her pocket. The lake gleamed like a shiny blue ribbon way down in front of them. "Today you're fourteen. How's it going, Billy?"

"I wish I had a different name." It bummed him out, it really did. "At least grown-ups like you call me Billy."

"Yeah? What do kids call you?" She brushed her wind-blown hair away from her face.

"What do you think? Belly Ehrendorf." He looked down at his gut. "Mom says I shouldn't eat so much. Dad says, as long as it's muscle. He got me some weight-lifting stuff. Kinda boring, though."

"Your dad's a big man," Julia said. Billy could see her looking at him, the way people did, to see how much he was like his dad. "I saw him in the grocery the other day. When you get as tall as he is, people won't be calling you names." She added, "You'll be okay. I bet you will." There was a pause. Then she grinned at him. "You Will. Me Julie. Happy birthday, Will."

Will Ehrendorf. Pretty cool, he thought, and couldn't help grinning back at her. That was neat, that a famous person could be so nice. And she'd remembered how old he was.

♫

Sharon told Mom, "All the girls are calling him Will."

He could feel his face getting hot and red.

His mother smiled across the dinner table. "All the girls?"

"About time, girls," Walt Ehrendorf said, reaching out to spear a pork chop from off of the platter. His hands were still blackened from work. "But forget about Willie wanka, boy. You're Bill. Had a hard enough time getting your mother to quit with William."

Mary Fran stopped smiling.

"It's too late," Sharon said. "Joanne'll never let it go."

That was for sure. Will counted on that. He'd figured

11

that if it got to Joanne Castle, who impulsively jumped on anything new, she'd never shut up, and pretty soon they'd all be used to it. Will. He'd said to Chrissy, who had the locker next to his, "Do me a favor. Call me Will." And being Chrissy the mouse-girl, of course she had called him Will, and she'd gone running, squeak, squeak, to Joanne. Now all he had to do was put up with Dad for a while.

"Will," said his mother thoughtfully, trying it out.

"Bill," his dad said firmly.

♪

## Then ~ Year 3

No Will Ehrendorf this year. That was fine with Julia. Cathy had told her about his new nickname. It had made her smile.

It was nice up here, by herself on the hill. Being ordinary. Without any problem family, or a major career, or even a priceless violin. No wonder the kid had thought she was grown up.

Not that she minded all of it. It was not all bad to be the brilliantly gifted Julia Levan, to have a lot of celebrity friends. And her family was fine in its weird kind of way, but sometimes she needed to take a break. She lay back on the flat gray granite, her sweatshirt bundled behind her head. She closed her eyes to the afternoon sun and breathed in the scent of grass and pine.

She had almost fallen asleep. She heard footsteps. Oh, well.

"Happy birthday, Will." She didn't open her eyes.

"My sister would kill me if she knew I was talking to Julia Levan." His voice was deeper this year.

"Whatever for? She could talk to me herself, if she hung out with Cathy."

"She would, but our Dad." He stopped, then continued in a rush, "Sharon's got this major thing for Phil Kavadas. All his band's albums and everything. She says you've been dating him. Is that true? Isn't he kind

13

of old for you?"

"He's thirty-two. I've known him for years. Yeah, we've gone out a couple of times

"Could you get his autograph for Sharon? Like, she joined his fan club and got the pictures and everything, but that isn't very personal. Her birthday's in October."

Julia said, "Philip keeps his private life and career – you know, fans and all – he keeps them really separate. So probably not." She opened her eyes and looked toward his voice. He was sitting cross-legged beside her.

"Wow," she said. "Have you grown up a lot or what? Fifteen's looking good on you."

"Yeah, I kinda have."

And kind of pleased with himself, too, she thought. She sat up.

He was looking a lot like his father, almost as tall and not much heavier. She thought that being like Walter Ehrendorf ought to be more of a compliment. It would be, if all that counted was dark-eyed good looks. If she didn't count the way Walt Ehrendorf looked at her when their paths crossed in the village, as though he knew something that she didn't know. As though he thought she'd be interested, unshaven and filthy as he was from his job on the County Road Commission, a man in his forties and going to fat. It made her feel as if she were prey, some harmless little animal who'd been spotted and stalked by a predator.

But that wasn't fair to Will. She'd seen Walt's son around the village all those summers before she started being away, and she'd talked to him since she'd started making a point of being up here on the hill on her

14

birthday each year. Will didn't strike her as a hostile, prejudiced jerk, assuming summer people were enemies, the way his father seemed to do. Or maybe assuming they were prey. This kid who came up here to the hill, the boy she talked to every summer, was not that bad a guy. Not bad at all.

♫

Late that September, Mary Fran Ehrendorf came in from the mailbox with a small square package addressed to Will.

She also had a warm peach pie, a gift from old Mrs. Hambrecht, Chrissy the mouse-girl's grandma. Mary Fran did stuff for the Hambrechts, helped them out around the house, helped them with business stuff. You'd think it would be somebody else who helped, their son or his large and bossy wife, or somebody from that holy roller church where they belonged. Mary Fran helped because she felt sorry for Chris, whose mother was dead and who had no father who'd ever been seen.

She invited all the Hambrechts for Saturday supper now and then. It got so his dad was always out those Saturday nights. Will saved his homework to work on then and was glad for Sharon to keep Chrissy company. 'Cause otherwise Chrissy would sit there watching him, her mouse-girl glances darting out from under long and limp colorless bangs, and his mother'd expect him to talk to her. How could he talk to someone so shy? He was glad Sharon was there to do it.

On her birthday a week later, his sister went totally goofy when she opened his present and saw the CD that wasn't even out in the stores, and right there on the liner was written, "To Sharon, Happy Birthday and many more, Sincerely, Philip Kavadas."

# CHAPTER TWO

### Now ~ Year 1

This evening's crop of recitalists, the fifth group of the summer, had larger, more enthusiastic families. They had also had time, by early August, to make friends among their fellow students. The performance shed was crowded, which was why Margaret found herself sitting uncomfortably close to the fat man in his two seats at the end of the row. He had been to every concert this year. Susanna sat to Margaret's left. The rest of the row was filled with a noisy clique of young women, all students. Susanna was uncomfortable too.

Don Jessup stood patiently on the stage, watching Henry fiddle with the microphone. Henry's white hair shone in the overhead lights. Kenneth Anderson sat in an aisle seat at the front. The director was clearly not as patient with delay as Donald Jessup was. At last, Henry unplugged the mike and carried the whole thing off the stage. A wise decision, Margaret thought.

The heavy man turned toward Margaret. His sleeve rubbed against the shoulder of her dress. There was no space between his body and hers.

"Are these kids tonight going to be really good?" He was tapping his right hand against his program.

"Of course," Margaret said automatically. Beside her, young Susanna stirred.

17

The fat man said, "That's what Kellie told me. I don't think she knows." He turned laboriously toward Margaret. "I asked her who you are, the lady who looks like she owns the place. My name's Will Ehrendorf," he said, and nodded.

Margaret bent her head in acknowledgment. "This is my friend, Susanna Hemelin," she said, including the girl beside her. "I trust Kellie told you I don't own the place."

Henry had returned to the stage. He was plugging in a replacement microphone.

Will Ehrendorf smiled. "Yeah, but she likes you better than she likes the big boss. Anyway." He shifted toward her again. "She brought me the program a couple days ago. I got some CDs of what's going to be on. By Itzhak Perlman and Hilary Hahn. Are these kids that good?"

Don Jessup had started to speak. Margaret put her finger to her lips.

Once in a great while, one of the summer music school students had both the talent and personality that might, if good luck held, lead to a solo career. Most were skilled enough to look forward to decent orchestra jobs. The school counted a dozen assistant concertmasters among its alumni, almost equal to Meadowmount, as Dr. Anderson had taken to saying, although Margaret knew that wasn't quite true. And a few were already struggling musically, pushed beyond their abilities by ambitious parents or unrealistic teachers who hoped they had found a prodigy, another Midori or Joshua Bell, or another Julia Levan. Margaret remembered

18

reading evaluations last summer, in Don Jessup's meticulous handwriting, before passing the forms to Kellie to file.

At intermission, when the gigglers in the rest of the row had rushed forward to crowd around their friends, Margaret gestured slightly to Susanna. The two moved over, leaving an empty chair between Margaret and the fat man. Will, he had said. She felt more comfortable now.

She turned toward him. "Our students are talented youngsters, but they don't have that kind of star power yet. If they did, they'd be performing at Tanglewood or Saratoga. Susanna's brother may turn out that way." She turned to smile at the girl.

"I wish," Susanna said, staring straight ahead. "Then I wouldn't have to get dragged up here. Next year, I'm gonna go work in my grandma's store."

"You are?" Will Ehrendorf leaned to see across Margaret. "What kind of store?"

"A grocery store. Not a supermarket," Susanna said. "A neighborhood independent, produce and meats, and a small selection of staples." Margaret stared at Susanna, unable to hide her amazement.

"No kidding," Will said. "That's the business I'm in. The Country Store, in Malburg Bay. You'd rather do that than be a musician?"

"I'm not the musician," Susanna said. "My brother is. His grandpa's a choir director and his grandma and dad are music teachers. That's how come he inherited talent. I'd rather be like Grandma Hemelin, leading a regular life."

19

Having delivered herself of this speech, Susanna slumped down in her chair and crossed her arms over her midriff. Her blue-jeaned legs ended in dirty tennis shoes that pushed the chair in front of her.

"Where's your grandmother's store?" Will asked. He produced a banana from one of his pockets and began to peel it slowly.

"Down in Cambridge," Susanna said to the chair she was staring at. "You ever been there?"

"No," he said. "I've been to Albany and Hillport. I go to Cumberland a lot."

My heavens, Margaret thought. The intermission was nearly over. She said to Will, "When our students perform, listen for tone and emotion. And look for technique and personality. It's always possible we're nurturing a future star, another Levan."

Susanna said, "I heard she lives around here. Julia Levan."

"So I understand. A summer home," Margaret agreed. "Dr. Anderson has invited her to visit the school. He hasn't had a reply." She glanced at Will Ehrendorf. "But you must know Julia Levan. She's probably come into your store." It seemed a rather remarkable thought.

"I know who she is," the fat man said.

A silence fell over their row.

♬

## Then ~ Year 4

"Can I ask you a kinda personal question?"

Something was bothering Will this year. Julia watched him where he sat beside her on the rock, his arms around his legs, his chin on his knees. Imitating her, she thought. He had done that before. He was staring moodily out at the view, his curls spilling down to his eyes. He was sixteen now.

"You can ask," she said. "I might not answer."

If he kept on losing weight as he grew, he was going to turn into some kind of hunk. She decided to forgive herself for what she was thinking. He was a nice kid.

"What's the question?"

"Is it true your father's a faggot?"

Oh, that. "Yeah, he is," she said. "Off and on."

"It doesn't bother you? That kind of sin?"

"It wouldn't, except for the headlines since he came out and people trying to tell me he's going to hell."

"He will," the boy said stubbornly. "He will, for doing things like that. He'll get the plague and burn in hell."

She turned on him. "I don't think so, Will. I know Edmund Levan, and I don't see an evil man. He has lots of friends. Some are gay. Sometimes they get together, is all."

"Promiscuity," he said.

"That's what hurt my mother," she agreed. "But lots

21

of guys do that to their wives. And girlfriends," she added. "Who with doesn't matter."

"Yes, it does. It's disgusting," Will said.

"What do you care? The worst that could happen, if some guy hits on you, just say no."

He shuddered. "Not me. I'm not like that." He looked at her in alarm. "You didn't think?"

"I didn't think anything, Will. You're starting to look like someone my dad's friends might ask. You don't have to hate them for asking. Just say no."

"Nobody better talk to me like that. There's no queers around here anyway, not any more."

"How do you know?" Besides, she thought, you're wrong. "What do you mean, any more?"

"There were a couple of guys used to be at school, Pete, and his buddy, Sam."

"And?"

"Randy and Jase and me, we kind of followed them. Snuck around behind Pete's house. They were sitting out on the deck and they got horsing around, like wrestling, you know what I mean? And Pete, he like kissed his buddy, right on the mouth. Sam, he got up and he kinda looked like something hit him. He walked away. Me and Jase and Randy, we took off up the hill. Jase puked in the woods, that's how bad it was."

"That's it? You never saw people kissing before?"

"Not guys!"

"And those are the queers who aren't here any more?" She looked out at the lake. "Where did they go?"

"Sam and his family, they moved away. Pete, well."

"Pete, what?"

"He killed himself last spring." Will's voice got scratchy. "Strung himself up from a tree out back of his house."

After a silence, Julia said, "What happened in between? When you saw him with Sam, and when he died?"

"Randy and Jase, they hassled him a lot, you know, like in the locker room."

"Randy and Jase. What about you?"

"They don't bother me any more, not since I stopped being so fat and got as tall as them."

"I meant, what did you do to Pete?"

"I wasn't in it, after a while. It was getting kinda rough."

Julia asked him quietly, "It bothered you? The way you and your friends were hating so much? That kind of sin? Driving a kid to suicide? Tell me something, Will. What are you going to do about it?"

♫

Just like his mother. No, he thought. His foot slipped on the edge of a rock. He righted himself and wiggled his ankle. Seemed to be okay.

She wasn't like his mom. Julia Levan would talk back when she thought something was wrong. And she wasn't awful, in spite of whatever her father might do.

23

What she was, was older than him. He'd never catch up. No matter how much time he spent wishing and waiting for August each year. No matter how many times he played her albums.

He was out of the woods, at the top of the field behind his house. The house where he kind of wished he didn't have to live.

Julia wasn't like his mom. She was braver. Her father was just as bad as his, he guessed, in a different way. At least she wasn't scared of her dad. He wondered if she ever had to decide, like he did, who to be like, her mom or her dad. Julia was probably more like her mom, the Fletcher side of her family, summer people who named their houses. The Fletchers' house was called Greenlea.

And that meant he'd never catch up. No daughter of the Fletchers would ever go for an Ehrendorf. He could just forget about it.

Right.

"As if," his sister Sharon would say.

♪

## Then ~ Year 5

"Cathy would kill me if she knew I was talking to Will Ehrendorf."

Julia sat down beside him. The wind was cold this afternoon. He was glad his mom's birthday present was a new sweatshirt.

"Mom told me Cathy's been down to the store every day this summer." She smiled at him. She looked tired. "I can see why. As the elders say, you are turning out well."

Will could feel his face getting red. "She's a nice kid, Cathy," he said. "But she's just a kid, like my sister, you know what I mean? I guess I kinda like older women."

She didn't say anything. He decided it was safe to look at her. She was staring out at the valley. Today, the lake was kind of gray and the mountains in Vermont were blue. Her long hair hung down along one side of her neck, like in the pictures with her violin on her new CD. She seemed to be almost frowning. He wanted to touch her hair.

He took a deep breath. "Those guys I told you about last year, Randy and Jase, you know?"

She nodded.

"They were starting to get on Pete's brother. He was a freshman last year, the brother, I mean, you know, Pete, the guy who..."

"I remember," she said. She seemed more interested

in the lake.

"I made 'em stop. Told 'em they'd have to go through me. I ended up getting into it with Randy, letting him know I could take him." He saw her making a little face. "Sometimes you gotta do that," he said. "My dad was real proud of me winning the fight. He wouldn't've been, if he'd've known why."

She didn't speak. Something was wrong.

"What's the matter?" He leaned toward her. "You ought to be happy, your birthday and all."

She shook her head. "Family problems. Nothing I want to talk about. What else have you been doing this year?"

"Well, working in the store. And, hey, I was on the track team, doing field events. I started running, on my own. This year I want to be a miler."

She smiled at that. "You doing track. I'd have thought you'd be on the football team."

He made a face himself. "They used to want me. Still do. Refrigerator Ehrendorf. Just because you used to look like it, doesn't mean that you want to play. Are you still dating Phil Kavadas?" There. It wasn't that hard to ask.

"I don't know," she said. "I haven't seen *People* magazine lately." He thought maybe she was teasing him. "A lot of that stuff is just to get folks to remember your name, to get it in print at the check-out lanes. He's still a friend. I've been going out with other guys too, people I knew at school."

Oh. "College guys," Will said.

"Yeah, ordinary guys like you. You'll be a college guy yourself a year from now."

"And you'll be graduated. Will you still come here in the summer time?"

"Well, sure. More," she said. "I mean, then I can concertize all year and not do so many summer festivals."

"You could live here all year long." He might see her somewhere besides this hill.

"I suppose, between tours, if I wanted to. But not for a while, anyway. The next few years, I guess I'll be staying close to New York."

"That'll be cool." Not for him.

"No, it won't. Oh, shit." She put her face down on her knees.

He wanted to touch her. "What's the matter?"

She raised her head. "You were right." She stared straight ahead. "My dad is positive."

"What about?"

She looked at him. "HIV positive. The virus. He's got it. It's turned into AIDS. In spite of the medications."

"Oh." He felt really funny. He opened and closed his hands. Hard. It didn't help.

"Last summer," she said, "I thought it was all so cool. Everything was about safe sex, no problem at all. I guess it was no problem, then. I didn't know. He's been positive for years and never told us and now he's getting sick. He had to go into the hospital yesterday." She glanced at him briefly and then looked away. "You were right, weren't you? He got the plague and he's burning

27

in hell and pretty soon he'll die." She closed her eyes and put her forehead down on her knees.

This is where it stops, Will thought. When I can't think of what to say and I get up and hike back down the hill and start in doing the chores. I'll be thinking about it and waiting for my birthday again, another whole year till August fourteenth.

He looked at her, hunched there on the rock, and he put out his hand and rested it on her back. She didn't move. Her hair was soft and silky straight. He moved over until his arm was around her, and then his other arm. She moved a little and leaned on him. She hadn't opened her eyes. She must think he was sorry for her about her dad. He kind of guessed he was. His face tingled where her hair touched it. She smelled so good. He reckoned he'd sit here and hold her a while and try to get used to how his body felt with her being really here, so close.

She was holding him too. Her hand was on his side. Under his sweatshirt. She slid it up to his shoulder and pushed him away, but her hand stayed there. She had opened her eyes. She looked at him silently, like he was sort of strange, he thought. It made him scared. She sat up straighter and leaned toward him and then she kissed him, gentle at first and then harder, and then her tongue was in his mouth. He finally figured out when to breathe. He reckoned he could kiss like that, and he did, even while she was leaning way back, pulling him down, her hands on his neck and running up and down his back, till she was lying on the ground and he was on top of her. Then she twisted her mouth away. She said, "I didn't bring protection. Did you?"

"You mean, like a...?"

He had never said that word to a girl before. He looked down at her and knew that he'd blown it. He had never even thought – well, maybe he had, but he didn't know, and Julia Levan was different.

"I mean like a condom," she said, "after what I've been telling you."

"No." He hated saying that. It wasn't what his dad would say.

She twisted away and sat up. He put his hand on her arm. He could tell from the way that she looked at him, she knew how strong he was.

She said, "I expect us to take good care of each other. We're friends, aren't we? I don't want to mess that up."

She stood up and walked a few steps away. He looked at his hand on the rock.

He said, "We could go now." He nodded toward the path he'd come up.

She bit her lip. "Where?"

He didn't have an answer for that. He stood up too. "Maybe, like, tomorrow?"

She looked him in the eye. "I'm going to visit my father tomorrow. You've never done any of this before, have you?"

He shook his head.

"I didn't think so. You catch on fast. I know it's not fair. I'm sorry I got so emotional."

"That's okay." He moved toward her. She took a step back. He stopped.

29

She said, "Maybe it's not such a bad first lesson, knowing you can stop when you should. When you have girlfriends, remember that."

"Julie." He'd never called her by name before. He couldn't even say it right.

"God, you are an adorable kid. I would hate not to do what's best for you. Happy birthday anyway, Will." She turned away.

"Next year," he called. "Next year, okay?"

She went down the hill without looking back. He thought, She didn't hear me.

He spun around and took off toward the top of the rock, into the trees and across to the other side.

Later, at dinner, when his mother was cutting his birthday cake, his father opened another beer and asked, "What happened to your hand?"

"I scraped it."

"I see that. How?"

"You want to know, taking a punch at a tree."

"You mind if I say it, you ain't real bright."

His mother said, "Walter." She was getting that tight, worried look on her face.

"Some people think I catch on fast."

"Yeah? Like who?" his father asked.

"Friends of mine."

"Randy and Jase," Sharon said. "I know who wishes you'd catch a clue. Joanne, that's who. And Chrissy Hambrecht, and who knows who else. Even rich bitch Cathy Levan, you know, that I used to play with. At least, that's what I heard."

"Joanne Castle?" His mother smiled. "Will, she's such a pretty girl."

Walter said, "And she don't think she's too good for my boy? What do you know about that?"

Will finished his cake. "Excuse me," he said to Mary Fran. His mother gave him a tired smile.

Out in the quiet twilight, he walked across the yard, not going much of any place. He heard his father's old pickup truck start.

Girlfriends, he thought. Now it wasn't just at school, it was even at home. Joanne and Chrissy and maybe Kellie. But he reckoned he wasn't in much of a rush, even if he was seventeen today and starting his senior year in two weeks. No law said you had to do anything. Girls like that, they'd be there, or other ones. He was doing better than any of them. He could wait and see another year, no matter what anyone said.

He jumped and grabbed the limb of the beech and swung and let go. He landed on his feet all the way down the slope, like he always had, ever since he was a kid. An adorable kid. Yeah.

♫

## Then ~ Year 6

Will thought he heard her. Then he was sure. He saw the top of her head, and her face, calm and peaceful like her pictures, not upset like she'd been last year. Maybe he should stand up, but he sat there beside the box wrapped in old green cloth. She came and sat beside him. The afternoon sun was warm.

"I brought you this," he said. "I reckon it's something you should have."

He picked up the object by his side and laid it on her lap. About the size of his mom's big kitchen cutting board, but thicker, maybe four inches thick. She unfastened the safety pins and pulled the fabric aside.

"I don't even know what it is," he said. "Except it makes music."

She lifted the lid off the wooden box. The metal strings inside stretched across the box and gleamed in the afternoon sun. A couple pegs didn't have any strings. He hadn't known what to do about that.

"Where did you get this?" Julia asked.

"My grandma's attic. She died last fall."

"Down there on the farm?"

"No, my Grandma Waterstone. She lived in Mayville, over by Lake Chautauqua, you know?"

"Ah, Chautauqua," Julia said.

She flicked a fingernail at one of the strings. Then she tilted the box up and ran her fingers across the pattern of inlaid wood around the outside.

"Did you find any hammers or sticks with it?" She flicked at a couple of strings again and listened to the plink they made. She twisted the pegs at the ends of the strings.

"Like a drum? No." The sound got better, he thought, like pretty water dripping. "Is that what you need to play it with?"

"Um." She was plucking the strings the way that Matt Stulsky played his guitar. He had never seen Julie look like that, wide-eyed and paying attention, like making the sound and listening was the neatest thing to do. Did she look like that when she played her violin? He thought, This is the best thing I ever did. Then he thought, That's the way she looked last year, just before she kissed me. After that, he wasn't sure what he was thinking.

"It's in great condition." She lifted up the box again, and this time she looked at the bottom. "Look at that. 'Grill, Lansing.' This might be really valuable, Will. Listen."

He listened because she had told him to. But mostly he watched her hands and her face. And the way she was moving slightly back and forth while she plucked the notes.

"It needs hammers," she said. She looked up. "You could find out over in Shelburne. Someone there could help you find where to get them."

He tapped the box with his knuckle. "What's it called?"

"It's a dulcimer. A hammered dulcimer. There are

33

other kinds, like lutes, you know, you play like a banjo. Those are mountain dulcimers. This is a hammered dulcimer."

"I want you to have it."

"You can't do that. This should stay in your family."

"But you have that old violin, right?"

"The Strad, yeah, but my grandmother bought that for thousands of dollars, from a man who couldn't play any more." She plucked at the strings, then put her hand on them to make them quiet. "If you sell this, it ought to go to someone who'll play it. Or a museum. It's valuable, Will."

"But I want you to have it. I want you to play it."

"No, Will, you can't give me this."

"I can if I want to. My mom said it's mine. I want you to have it. I love you, Julie."

She raised her hands from the strings. Then she placed the dulcimer carefully on the rock and she turned to face him.

"Will, we're friends. Don't think it's anything more than that."

Her face was so serious. This was something big. He didn't really understand. He thought, Every summer there's been more. He didn't know how he had been so wrong.

He reached out and touched her very gently. She didn't say no. Then he leaned and kissed her, like she did to him last year. It didn't get harder, more intense. Instead, she pulled away. He didn't know what it was he'd done wrong.

"Where's this place that isn't all rock?"

"What?"

She had jumped to her feet. "You did come prepared?" she asked. She sounded angry.

He nodded. His hands were shaking.

"Good. But just in case, so did I."

♫

It was getting dark and getting cold. She ought to go home. Julia sat on the park bench at the swimming beach. Someone had moved the bench close to the edge of the lake. The water had darkened along with the sky. Its tiny wavelets made gentle lapping sounds near her feet.

She could start for the city tonight. The city was far away from the country, and far away from young country boys. Remember that, Julie, she said to herself. A one-hour friendship once a year up on the hill. Only eighteen, but he'd turned out to be something special. Maybe. Not likely. A kid, a boy she really knew nothing about. Get a grip, she said to herself. You made a fool of yourself today. You don't have to do it again.

She wouldn't wait for the one last holiday weekend, for Mom and Cathy to come back over from Hillport. She could stay at the hotel in Saratoga tonight and be down in the city by tomorrow afternoon.

She'd go down to the city and visit her dad. Then a last semester, eight more credits. She would stick to

35

that. In the new year, she'd come back to New York and make up her mind about Phil's proposition. In the city, what he had asked wouldn't seem too bizarre. She stretched her legs, then pulled them back and stood up.

"Leavin' so soon?" a deep voice asked behind her. She spun around. Walter Ehrendorf stood there in the darkened night. "Just when I got here?"

"What do you want?"

"You like this place, don'cha?" He gestured toward the park and the lake with a large hand wrapped around a can. Beer, she thought.

"Yes," she said. "Good night." Her car was a hundred feet away. She started for it.

He grabbed her arm. "Don't be so fast."

"Let go of me!"

"You don't have to go."

"Yes, I do! Let go of my arm." He was drunk, Julie thought.

"Just looking out for you, girl. Never know who's hanging out around here."

She'd never seen anyone in the park in an early evening, except that teenage couple one time. She looked around. There was no one else here.

"Then I better go home. Let go of my arm."

"Too good for me, that what it is?" His beery breath was too close to her face. "Fool kid of mine, got them fancy records of yours. Wasting his time, what I say. Pretty stuck-up rich girl like you, wouldn't give him time of day. Or either his dad. Don't know what you're missin', girl. You wanna find out?"

Through the leaves, she could see lights in the houses up on the hill. She sucked in a chestful of air and opened her mouth. Her knee came up and rammed into Walter Ehrendorf's crotch.

He grunted in shock. His grip loosened. She spun and ran and started screaming, as loud as she could. She got to the car and grabbed at the door. Her hands shook. The key went in the ignition at last. Walt was straightening up, stumbling towards her. The engine started. The wheels snarled on gravel and screeched on the road.

No headlights behind her. She'd be all alone at the summer house. She looked at the gas; the tank was three-quarters full. She made a U-turn at the fork. Down to the bridge and across the lake, and she wouldn't stop until Hillport.

♫

"I expect us to take good care of each other." It didn't always work that way.

It was February before he got up the nerve and the money for the museum. The museum lady sent him to the library, and the library lady, looking over the top of her glasses, sent him up to the university library, and the guy at the university, Rob, a tall young guy with a wispy beard and glasses that were perfectly round, sent him down to the music store. And there, Marnie, the girlfriend of the library dude, stopped talking with her grungy friends and got interested in the problem of

37

sticks for a hammer dulcimer. And this older lady with long gray braids said she got a magazine, and she happened to have one here in her bag, which Will thought might hold everything the lady owned, and there was an ad for dulcimers. A photocopy of the ad was in his shirt pocket now.

He stared into the tunnel his headlights made in the driving snow and hoped he was somewhere near the right lane of the bridge.

It took him more than two hours to get up to Malburg Bay from the bridge. It was dark. He was late for dinner.

But not late enough, he thought when he saw the Hambrechts' car in the drive next to his mother's. It hadn't been there very long; there wasn't much snow drifted on it. He should have taken his time and missed dinner. And then he saw the other car, the State Police car, kind of sideways off the edge of the drive. That was funny, if his dad's friend, Al the trooper, was staying for dinner too. Lights were on all over the house.

He stomped his feet on the porch to knock off the snow. His mom would understand, coming in the front door, as long as he didn't track snow. He wondered what they were having for dinner.

Funny how he remembered wondering that, about dinner, how he remembered that whole evening for so long, and the sick kind of feeling that started when the big man in uniform, Al McGreevy, his father's friend, stood up from the ottoman where he'd been sitting and leaning toward Mary Fran, stood up and turned to Will and said, "Son."

# CHAPTER THREE

### Now ~ Year 1

Susanna said, "Well, excuse me, Margaret. I was just being honest." She turned to Will Ehrendorf, who was sitting opposite her, overflowing his chair at Margaret and Henry's dining table. "Didn't you ever have to take music lessons?  Did you hate them?" she asked hopefully.  It was early August, two weeks from the end of this summer's music school.

"Yes and yes," Will replied. "Piano, for a little while. A couple of months. My mother's idea. It wasn't pretty."

Margaret smiled in spite of herself.

"Yeah, piano," Susanna said. "At least that's better than violin. But I'd rather guitar, if I have to."

"Indeed," Henry said so benevolently that Margaret suspected he hadn't heard the entire exchange. "There's some lovely work for violin and guitar," Henry said. "Rodrigo. Joaquin Rodrigo."

"My folks don't want to schlep to more than one teacher," Susanna said. "And they get a sibling discount too. I keep trying to tell them, they'd save a hundred percent on the second kid if they'd let me stay home."

"Fifty percent," Will said.

Susanna made a face.

Margaret stood to clear the plates. Susanna jumped

up to help. "Let's sit over," Margaret prompted Henry, nodding in the direction of the cabin's living room.

In the kitchen, Susanna said, "Margaret, this is so cool. A dinner party. The girls in the dorm think it's weird. I love it. So, what do you think? I thought he had a family."

"I thought so too," Margaret replied.

♪

## Then ~ Year 7

When she reached the top, on the open rock the rain was falling steadily. How appropriate, Julia thought. She pulled up the hood on her rain jacket.

He was waiting. He stood under a tree, huddled inside his own jacket. She kept her distance. She wanted to reach out and touch his arm.

"Are you all right?"

It took him a while to answer. "Pretty much," he finally said.

"Ah, Will. Your dad. Your sister." She wanted to hold him. "You married Chrissy Hambrecht."

"Yeah, well, she's having a baby," he said. He looked at her defiantly. "I wasn't real bright. I didn't remember the lesson," he said. He'd thought he had. He was wrong.

Julia turned away. "Who would? You need someone, Will. You must have a lot do for your mother."

He looked down the hill at the tops of the trees. He nodded. What he had to do for his mom was just be quiet, forever. Not tell anyone, even Julie who knew about what happened to Pete, Julie whose father behaved pretty bad himself.

Not ever talk about the report that came to his mother in the mail and he heard her stuff it in that drawer when he came back to the kitchen. He sat there and waited until she went away. Then he got it out and

41

read about how they had examined Dad and counted the fractures in his skull and listed all the broken bones and damaged organs. Then there was another report, the one about Sharon, almost exactly the same kind of thing but he read it all anyway, even where it said at the end that she had been two months pregnant. He put the papers back in the drawer and shut it quietly. He reckoned his mother would tell him, if she wanted him to know. He thought she burned the papers that night. She never said a word.

"Cathy told you what happened?" he asked. How else would Julia know?  She was never here.

"When she heard about it in June." She looked out at the wall of cloud. "What would you like for a wedding present?"

"From you?" Silence then. "Nothing."

She said, "I understand. Happy birthday, Will."

She turned and walked away from him, stepping carefully on the slippery rock. She stopped and turned.

"It would be better," she said, then took in a breath. "Don't come up here any more, Will."

He could hear her uneven steps down the hill for a long time. When he couldn't hear her any more, it was time to go. But he stood there, saying it all in his head, what he hadn't been able to say out loud. You knew what my dad was like. You were supposed to understand, he thought. You said you did, but you didn't.

His own life had somehow skidded off the road.

42

♫

"Package, miss," Robert the doorman said. Julia frowned at the large square box. Loving hands at home had made the box out of a larger carton and then been generous with the tape. She peered at the address label. Ehrendorf, Malburg Bay. She should send it back. She asked Robert to bring the box to the seventh floor.

She lifted the dulcimer out of its bubble-wrapped bed and pushed the box to the floor. When the inlaid top came off, she saw a handsome notecard, a lakeshore scene, fitted under the strings. Inside, in a careful neat hand, was written, "I want you to have this. Will."

She should send it back. Instead, the next day, she went to the bookstore and found an equally handsome card, the New York City skyline at dawn, and wrote "Thank you" neatly inside. Three days later, she mailed the card.

43

♫

## Then ~ Year 8

He sat at the top of the hill, pretty far back from the edge of the cliff. The end of the baby harness was looped around his arm. At the other end of the strap, Stephanie was crawling on the rock. She'd been doing that most of the afternoon. Sometimes she struggled to her feet and practiced walking. Sometimes she sat and played with her toys. He had only had to change her once. Her hands were dirty, and the knees of her pink overalls were scraped, and the toes of her tiny sneakers.

People made such a big deal about how much she looked like him. "The spitting image of your daddy, aren't you, Steffi?" they'd say. Chrissy just closed her eyes when they did, the way she had when she'd first seen her newborn. He reckoned it didn't matter to Stephanie. None of what had happened had been her fault. She was a sweet little girl. She would be in big trouble if all she had was Chris. He'd be there while Steffi needed him. He figured he owed it to Sharon too.

But only Steffi. And only while she needed him. He reckoned he might get careless again, or maybe get lied to again. He'd taken care of that. The doctor had asked him if he was sure. He was sure.

His mom said half the insurance was his. After he bought the used trailer house and he'd gone over to Hillport to that Dr. Patric, he put the rest in the bank. "You should use it to start taking courses at night," his mother said. She had been to college; she taught first grade. She had always planned that he and Sharon

44

would go to SUNY too.

Things were different now. That money could sit there, earning interest, and someday Steffi would go. It bothered his mom a lot. "Will," she said, "you could do so much with a college degree. Your father's life was so limited. I want you to do better than that."

He thought doing better wouldn't be hard. He hoped, he hoped. Sometimes it scared him so much, he almost got sick, thinking he might do something like that. He should have stopped it. Maybe he could have. After all, he'd beaten up Jase. He could have gone in there and said, "Don't you ever touch her again," or gotten the rifle from out of the barn. Or something. But he hadn't, and now look. He guessed he deserved it. Maybe they all deserved it. All but Sharon.

Stephanie was on her feet, toddling toward him. "Dada," she said. Her face was rosy. He wondered if he'd kept her out in the sun too long. He should have thought of that before.

"Say 'Happy birthday, Will'," he said to the black-eyed little girl.

She said, "Dada." She tripped, and before he could catch her, she fell flat on her face on the rock.

Now he'd done it. He picked up the crying baby. Her nose was dirty. It wasn't very badly scratched. He held her against him, his hand much bigger than the back of her curly dark head.

"I guess she meant it," he said to Stephanie. "I reckon we can stop hanging around." He picked up the knapsack that held all her baby stuff. "Come on, Gretel.

Let's head back to the cage." He would take her home and he would go run, get it out of his system.

♫

"What have you decided?" Philip's arm lay the distance between them along the back seat of the car. He lifted the ends of her hair and let the strands slide down through his fingers.

She sighed and pulled her gaze away from Fifth Avenue in the September rain. The night streets as they passed were laced with jeweled ribbons, reflected lights from buildings and cars glistening on the wet pavement. "Sure, why not?"

"Sure, why not," Philip repeated quietly. His fingertips stroked her hair.

His eyes were invisible behind the silver-lensed aviator glasses he always wore when he went out, whenever he was not hidden away behind his own gates and doors.

"There's nothing between us," she said. That was the reason why not.

"Yes, there is. But not what anyone would expect."

"Not what anyone would expect," she agreed. "Your people will take care of it all?" She turned her eyes back to the passing streets.

"All you have to do is show up."

# CHAPTER FOUR

### Now ~ Year 2

"Look, Margaret," Susanna said. "Orders." She waved sheets of paper in Margaret's direction from the door of Margaret's office.

"Susanna, you didn't," Kellie said, peering over the girl's shoulder, then giving Margaret a worried glance.

"So, can I use your computer?" Susanna asked Kellie. "My supplier can have all these items here in ten days."

The girl had lost some of her pre-teen weight. Margaret was relieved to see that Susanna this summer looked a confident fourteen but did not appear to be going on thirty, as many of the young women students seemed to do.

"But Dr. Anderson said..." Kellie said.

"I know what he said," Susanna retorted. "He was right, too. The store loses money." She tapped the papers in her hand. "But this isn't to stock the shelves. This stuff is already sold. Seven sweaters, a dozen sweatshirts, two dozen mugs, fifty music portfolios. It'll never rot in that closet they call a store. Margaret and I figured it out. Jenny Beth, my supplier, already has the logo."

"It's all right, Kellie," Margaret said. "I forgot to tell

47

you about the custom order arrangement. We hope it will make some money for the school this year. And give Susanna something to do."

"You sure it's okay with him?" Kellie asked.

Margaret wasn't at all sure, but she nodded anyway. They were two weeks into the summer session. Susanna's mother was back with Jordan. Grandma Hemelin was ill, so Susanna had had to come back too. Margaret had exchanged many emails with the girl, and with Dr. Anderson, persuading him that Jordan Kesto was destined to be a star alumnus and therefore his tag-along sister should be accommodated. In the end, Margaret had gotten her way. She knew there would be a price to pay.

♬

## Then ~ Year 9

"Christine." Marilyn Hambrecht pushed back her chair and stood up. She was a tall, big-boned woman with a pockmarked face.

Chrissy, still reed-thin and still washed out, got up from the Thanksgiving dinner table and followed her aunt into the kitchen. Will's mother, and Bonnie and Marcy, Chris's cousins, knowing what was expected of them, scraped back their chairs and began clearing dishes. Will stayed where he was, with two-year-old Stephanie on her booster seat beside him. Old August Hambrecht coughed, glanced at his wife, then leaned on his cane and struggled to his feet, leading his son, Art the accountant, and his teenage grandson Tom toward the television in the front room.

"'Mon, Daddy," Steffi said, sliding off her chair and tugging him toward the television.

Lydia Hambrecht was still sitting at the table. When she had finished the last of her pie, Will knew, the old lady would make her way out to the kitchen to supervise. When the dishes were washed and wiped and put away, the day would be over. The women would troop into the living room, and Marilyn, with Lydia beside her and Chrissy almost hiding in the background, would announce that it was time to go home. In the same big voice she had used three years ago to inform Will and Mary Fran that Will would have to marry Christine.

49

Even though he thought it was Chrissy's fault. She'd started it, waking him up in his room that afternoon a month after the accident. Chrissy the mouse-girl. Who would've thought? But it wasn't right to blame her. That would only make it worse for his mom, with her tired eyes and her hair getting gray. And Chrissy was desperate, he'd seen it in her eyes, desperate not to be what her family expected, a tramp, a slut, like her mother had been.

"'Mon, Daddy," Steffi said.

♫

## Then ~ Year 12

"The cause was AIDS," Kellie read, "according to his daughter, the violinist Julia Levan. She is the wife of Philip Kavadas." Kellie and Chris were sitting at the scarred old dining table between the little kitchen and the trailer's living room.

"But, get this," Kellie said to Christine. "At the end, it says, 'In addition to his daughter Julia, he is survived by his wife, Elinor Fletcher of Hillport, Vermont, a second daughter, Catherine Levan of Hillport, and a grandson, Alexander Kavadas.'"

"What about it?" Will stood at the sink, watching five-year-old Stephanie in the back yard, playing with Ashley Brent. Seven years, he thought. Edmund Levan had had the plague for seven years.

"That's pretty weird, isn't it, Chrissy?" Kellie said. Two-month-old Jared Brent was asleep in his baby carrier on the floor. "I always thought they must be divorced, Cathy and Julia's parents. I mean, if Jason walked out on me, I'd have his butt in court so fast. And this guy" – Kellie tapped on the newspaper – "dying of AIDS? Who would stay married to someone like that? It gives me the creeps, just thinking about it," Kellie said, shuddering. "Cathy always seemed pretty normal."

Chrissy said, "Maybe they got married in church."

"Huh?" said Kellie.

That was Chrissy, Will thought. A quiet little mouse of a girl, keeping things to herself till she blurted them

51

out and you didn't know what she was talking about. She'd wanted to get married in church, that strange roadside church in the old schoolhouse that her family's life revolved around. Will had said no, they'd find a judge. That would be more honest, he'd said.

"You know, in sickness and health, till death do us part?" Chrissy said now. "Maybe she keeps her promises, Cathy's mom."

"Forsaking all others, too, you know," Kellie pointed out. "If he didn't do that, why should she? Life's too short, or maybe too long."

"You got that right," Will said.

Steffi was sitting in her sandbox outside, showing Ashley Brent how to upend a sand-packed bucket to make a row of towers.

That was good, Kellie's attitude. It was good for Chris, spending time with Kellie. Keep that in mind. Life is too long.

"Anyway," Kellie said, "can you imagine finding out that your husband is – queer? I mean, Jase is no angel, but we get along. But if I ever ever found out anything like that – not that I would, not Jason Brent – he would never come within twenty feet of me again. And I'd never let him near the kids."

Well, that was it, Will thought. Whatever he did, it had to be bad enough to make Chris want to leave, but not so bad that Stephanie would get hurt or that he wouldn't be able to look after Steff.

"What a fantastic day," Kellie said, stretching and glancing out the window. "I was thinking spring would never come. Those daffodils next door are gorgeous. So many of them," she said to Chris. "Your mother-in-law must spend a lot of time on her garden."

"Will does it," Chrissy said. "He takes care of everything around her house, don't you, honey?"

He nodded. Chris added, "It means he doesn't have time to do much around here." She looked around the narrow mobile home. It was used when he bought it and now it was showing its age. The new couch kind of stood out, a Christmas present from his mom.

"You know what I think?" Chris said to Kellie. "I think Mary Fran ought to think about moving. She could get a teacher job anywhere." Chris had said this a dozen times to Will. "She should be somewhere where she could meet people. You know, maybe some nice man who lost his wife? She's not so old, and I know she's lonely. And then we could have that house."

Will said, "No, we couldn't. She'd have to sell it. We can't afford to buy it."

"We could if you'd get a better job. You'd get paid twice as much if you worked for the county. You know Ed Richards would give you a job like the one your father had."

Kellie was looking interested. She had not heard all this before.

Chrissy said, "I know you like the Hermans, like the store, but they don't pay you anything, Will. That's the exact same job you had in high school, only now you do it full-time. If you like the grocery business so much, you should get a job with Gilson's. You'd get promotions and benefits. They even pay for going to school."

"I don't want to drive that far." Dumb, but that was

53

what he always had to say about it.

"You don't want to drive that far. Then how come every Wednesday you disappear up to Cumberland?"

"I disappear on Wednesday because that's when the library's open late." Same old answer as every time.

He thought Kellie looked like she didn't believe it. He knew Chrissy almost didn't. Her and her stuff about promises. She had gotten what she needed. He knew she thought he might be seeing someone up there. He wasn't. What he had said about the library, that was the simple truth. Just not all of it.

♫

"Julie, dear, I think we're ready," Elinor said.

Emilia came over and picked up the boy. "Time for nap, Alex. Say, 'Bye-bye, Mama, Grandma, Aunt Cathy.' See you later, Miss Julie." She carried Alex off to his room.

Julia stood up and straightened her black suit and reached into her bag for her sunglasses. In the hall, waiting for the elevator, the three women were silent. Julia's arm was around her sister's shoulder.

Their mother said, "I do think Philip should have come."

Julia said, not for the first time, "It's better not, Mom. He's right, it would turn it into a circus."

Cathy said, "It'll be a circus anyway."

"But he's family, Julie," Elinor protested. "Not to be

with his wife at her father's funeral. What kind of family is that?"

"You mean, what will the public say? They can say whatever they like. We have no obligation to explain." Julia sighed. "I spent all those years being asked if I was a 'normal' kid in spite of being a prodigy. And in spite of you and Dad being separated but not divorced, when everybody knew about Dad. Grandmama is right, you know. There is no such thing as a normal person, and if there were, no law says anyone has to be it. It's just an excuse for the chattering classes to talk."

"My sister, the cynic," Cathy said.

Julia smiled and hugged her. "Your sister, the celebrity. Better to be cynical than to take ourselves too seriously."

"You got that from Grandmama, too," Cathy said.

"But of course. You and Mom are my ballast, she's my anchor to windward. Without you all, I would have gone under a long time ago. Can you imagine if Dad and Philip had been my only influences?"

Even Elinor had to smile.

Julia thought of Philip, out at the house in Connecticut, working on new material to record, not appearing in public today, as he never would again, not even to honor his father-in-law and closest friend, the late Edmund Levan.

55

♬

## Then ~ Year 13

He wished Joanne would cut it out. He stood at the cash register and watched her climb out of her old green Ford. It was hot outside at the end of August. There was no reason for Joanne to be shopping here. Wasn't even all of her shopping, probably. When she got back up to Toctin, she'd be stopping by the supermarket.

It wasn't that she wasn't attractive, with her generous body and her open round face and ready smile. She hadn't let Tommy's fooling around mess her up too badly; she went out and got a job with the county, and her neighbor kept the kids after school. And she looked around. The only thing was, who was there her own age to date? The only good ones were already married or they'd already moved away. He knew how they thought, Joanne and Kellie. But at least they tried. He wished some of that trying would rub off on Chris. Then maybe someone else would find her.

Joanne came in here because of Will. The Hermans ought to pay him extra for that. She left her kids somewhere and she came over to pick up some things, she said. And to talk to Will, to remind him that Tommy Brent was gone, moved to Lake Placid with the latest girlfriend, and that Joanne's divorce was final. And to see if any of it was true, what Kellie, Joanne's sister-in-law, had told her, that Will and Chris were having trouble.

Chrissy was having trouble, maybe. He could see as well as anyone how she was losing her pale blonde not-

56

quite-prettiness. He knew people said how tired she looked, how washed-out she was getting. Let it happen. He couldn't live Chrissy's life.

Steffi was in school now. She was six, going into first grade, in his mother's classroom. But Chris kept hanging around the house, thinking she couldn't do anything else, because maybe she'd have another baby or maybe someday she'd have to take care of a bigger house than the trailer.

You would think by now Chrissy would have figured it out, that if she wanted anything more, she was going to have to get it herself. He wouldn't tell her, because he knew if they started talking, pretty soon they'd be almost yelling – he would be yelling, anyway – and Chris would go quiet and tight with anger she wouldn't or couldn't express, and he didn't want Steffi living with that. This way, he kept himself out of it.

♫

Julia wiped down the violin and placed it back in the case. Last summer, she'd woken up to the CBC in Ottawa in time to hear Peter Tonyea call the Barber concerto "tortured sweetness." The announcer was right. She snapped the latches and looked out the long window at the end of the austere oblong practice room. To the north, the green hills of Litchfield County rolled and rose toward the Berkshires. Alex would be waking up from his nap pretty soon. It was still quite warm outside, in mid-September. She and Alex could have a swim.

"Mommy, look." It was an hour later. She swam toward the boy.

Her son dropped a rock into the pool and flopped on the edge to peer down at his treasure on the bottom. What was it with boys and splashing? Julia knew the drill. She bent into the water and dove like a seal for the rock. Alex grabbed the offering from her opened hand and pitched it as far as he could. He would have gone on playing fetch for an hour. She ducked her head back to sluice her hair out of her face.

"Julia. Miss Levan." It was Karen, Philip's nurse.

"Karen?" But she knew. She climbed the ladder and reached her robe in three quick steps.

"You'd better come."

"Yes," Julia said. "Alex." She scooped up the boy in a towel. "Sweetie, come on. We have to go in."

"No, Mommy." He tried to wriggle out of her arms.

"Alex, hush. Daddy needs us. We have to go in."

♫

## Then ~ Year 13

Things were slow this hot afternoon. A lot of the summer people weren't here yet. There was no one in the store. Will picked up his Walkman. He reckoned he'd finish pricing those cans.

He heard the door slam. From where he was at the end of the far corner aisle, he heard voices. A woman with a little kid. Probably Donna Herman and her youngest, Mikey. Donna drove the ten miles from where she and Greg lived, almost next door to Gilson's, to shop in her in-laws' market. Dumb, but nice, keeping it in the family. Nobody had ever figured it out, why Mike and Angela kept on going with the store, such a crappy shoestring little business. Not even Will had it figured out, and he was almost running the place. Oh, well, he thought, no one had ever figured out why he had never quit. He wasn't going to tell them.

It couldn't be Donna who had come in. Donna would have called his name. He put the labeler down on the box. He'd better go see if they needed help.

Julia Levan was in the aisle where the cereals and cookies were. It took his breath away that it happened like that, it really did, seeing her standing there in his store, in jeans and T-shirt just like before, not looking any different. Her hair was still long and straight, that dark, dark brown with a little red.

She turned her head slowly and smiled. "Hi, Will. We came to get some Cheerios. Gotta have 'em, don't we, Alex?" She spoke to the little boy standing beside her. "Alex, this is my friend, Will."

Will thought the boy looked like her, with his straight hair and big brown eyes. "What kind of Cheerios?" he asked. Then he said, "I was sorry to hear about your husband. You've had a tough couple of years."

"Yes, we have," Julia said with a gentle smile. She looked at Will. "Dying takes such a damned long time, or no time at all. Anyway, it's over. I guess I can't say things are back to normal. I don't think I've ever known normal. At least they've quieted down."

Chrissy had said Julia looked old and tired and sad on the TV news last fall, coming out of the pretty Greek church with her mother and Cathy after the service for Philip Kavadas. She didn't look old or tired now, or even very sad. He thought she looked wonderful.

"Your mother's not here yet," he said for something to say, as if she didn't know. "I haven't seen your grandmother. But I met your sister's husband. Cathy looks pretty happy."

"She is," Julia agreed. "Malcolm's a nice guy. Mom's not over here very much." She smiled. "She's got a new man in her life. It's kind of a complicated situation. But Grandmama, well, she's eighty-five. She doesn't get out very much at all. She's really starting to fail.

"Alex, sweetie, don't touch," she said. She bent over and looked at the shelf with him. "Which cereal do you want?" The boy pointed up, and Will took the box off the shelf. "What about you, Will? How are you and your wife?"

"I guess we're fine." He felt stupid and uncomfortable. But if he just stood there and looked at her, and thought about how she had been on the hill, that would be worse.

The door of the store opened again. Stephanie came skittering in and danced down the aisle in her halter top and her shorts, her arms outstretched, tapping the cans and boxes on the shelves on either side. She always did that. He was always surprised that nothing ever got knocked off.

Christine was behind her. "Stephanie Amber Ehrendorf," Chris called. "Slow down and be polite." Steffi stopped short in front of Julia Levan. Chris stopped at the end of the aisle.

"This is my daughter, Steffi," Will said. "Steffi, this is Julie and Alex. Hey, Chris, come here." She did, reluctantly. "You remember Chrissy, don't you?" he asked Julia. "From when she and my sister were friends with Cathy?"

"Of course, but that was ages ago." Julia smiled and nodded to Chris. Steffi was holding a hand out toward Alex, and he was deciding if he wanted to pretend to be grown up. He decided not and closed the gap between himself and his mother.

"We just came in for milk and eggs," Chrissy said. "It's nice to meet you, to see you again," she said to Julia. "Stephanie, come on."

Julia stood with her hand on her son's shoulder and watched Chris walk away. Then she turned her head and smiled at Will. She said, "You don't climb Rocky Knob any more."

61

And that took his breath away again, but deeper down this time, because how would she know a thing like that?

He had gone to Cumberland yesterday. It was Wednesday, why not? Chris had said, "You shouldn't do that, honey," so he had told her he would come home for lunch first. They could have a birthday party then, if she wanted to make a fuss.

And then he had gone to Cumberland. His friend Rob, the librarian, had made a plan of what he should read. He was getting to the end of the books about psychology, the stuff he read while Chris watched TV. It was pretty interesting. And sometimes funny. Like that story about the lady whose husband complained she never wanted to have sex. The shrink had looked at the man, very fat and not very clean, and basically said to the wife but in longer words, "Well, who would?"

He reckoned he'd get some books about the grocery business after he finished psychology. But now, today, he was standing here in the aisle next to Julia Levan. Chrissy was coming back with her milk and eggs, Stephanie beside her. Chris put down her basket and stood beside him, holding his arm.

Julia said to Alex, "Maybe we'd better get some bread," and Steffi said, "In the next aisle. Alex and I can get it, huh?" To Will's surprise, Alex followed his daughter.

Julia said to Chris and Will, "You might be able to help me. You know Mrs. Warren, who's looked after our house all these years?"

They nodded. "She goes to our church," Chris said.

"She's getting on herself. I was wondering, do you know someone younger we could get to help? To be Mrs. Warren's assistant? She'll still want to do it. She's a dear and a wonderful cook, and she's so conscientious. I thought, if Cathy and I suggest getting someone to help, we'd better be specific."

"Gee, I don't know," Chris said, looking up at Will. He knew, immediately, but it wouldn't help to blurt it out.

He said, "Someone's going to want that job. What we could do is let people know. If anyone's interested, we could tell them to call you."

"Call Cathy. She's over in Hillport. That would be wonderful," Julia said. "I'm so glad I thought to ask you." She smiled, mostly at Will.

He remembered that smile, and thought about it, all afternoon, and that evening while he was running, and later, hurting Chrissy's feelings because he wanted to be alone and she was in the mood again.

He wasn't going to lie to Chris. It was bad enough, the stuff they didn't talk about, because it all went back to what had happened before. If they talked about it, they couldn't act like they were normal for Stephanie's sake, like this was a regular family.

He never went up that hill any more. Why make himself miserable? And now look, he got to see Julia anyway. He might have not gone to Cumberland yesterday. It had been a sort of special birthday, twenty-five. But Stephanie was just turning seven. It was still too soon. Steffi needed him and her mom.

♬

Julia sat in the car at the top of the drive and watched Alex walk down toward the family on the porch. He was carrying the grocery bag, almost as big as himself. Cathy and Malcolm had arrived, with two-month-old Alyssa. Elinor was sitting out on the porch with them, holding her granddaughter on her lap.

The porch needed painting and so did all the outside trim. The house was well over a hundred years old and needed constant attention. She'd call tomorrow and arrange to have it done in September, when the family had all gone home but before the first snow.

Family, Julia thought as her boy reached the porch. You have yours, and I have mine. That's how it is. It never would have worked anyway. We'd both have too far to go, to meet in the middle. She sighed.

Besides, in this family, things don't last, she thought. People don't last. Remember that, she said to herself, getting out of the car.

# CHAPTER FIVE

### Now ~ Year 2

"You're worried about Susanna, aren't you?" Will Ehrendorf stood in the aisle of the dilapidated grocery store, his enormous body filling the space between the shelves, turning to speak quietly to Margaret. Susanna had gone on to the end of the aisle and turned the corner, as if she were on an inspection tour.

"Yes, I am. I like the child. Apparently, her grandmother's quite ill, and she may not be able to spend next summer in Cambridge after all. The grocery store is going to be sold. She's done nothing but read and kill time all this summer. I can't see it another year."

A short man with steel-gray hair pushed through a plastic curtain from a back room.

"They'll be back next year, her mother and her brother?"

Margaret nodded. It was mid-August. The summer school would be closed up next week.

Will smiled at someone behind Margaret. She turned. It was Kellie Brent.

"Mrs. Renfrew," Kellie said in surprise. "I didn't know you shopped over here."

"I don't usually," Margaret said. "Susanna and I were

65

out for a drive. This is rather out of my way."

She hoped the disclaimer was tactful enough. Outside the store when they arrived, she and Susanna had frowned at each other. Now that Margaret had seen the inside, the dirty-looking wooden floor, the harsh light, the old fixtures that made the stock look old too, she didn't know how she ought to feel, appalled or merely distressed.

"Did you hear about Cathy?" Kellie said to both of them. Will nodded somberly. "It's so sad," Kellie said.

"A friend?" Margaret asked.

"Cathy Tennant," Kellie said. "Cathy Levan. They moved her to a nursing home this morning. She's had MS for a long time. Multiple sclerosis," she added.

"Cathy Levan?" Margaret asked.

"Julia's sister," Kellie said.

"Then she must be quite young. What a tragedy," Margaret said sympathetically.

"How's Chrissy?" Kellie asked Will.

"Okay, I guess. Stephanie said she was."

"Chrissy's staying, then? To help the Levans?"

"She's almost part of the family," Will said. "That's what they keep telling me when I go to pick her up."

"Yeah, that's what everyone says." Kellie reached to take a box from the shelf. An excuse to come here, Margaret thought. "In its way, it's a blessing," Kellie said. Will nodded again.

In the car outside, Susanna said, "He's a stock clerk. I thought he said it was his store. Those old people, that man, they own it."

"Um," Margaret said. To get out of their parking space, it was necessary to back up a grade.

"Three cars in this parking lot, and all I bought was a candy bar. You call that volume?" Susanna sounded outraged. "I can't believe I had such a wrong impression, you know? And it's not a big mark-up, I'll tell you that. No add-ons, either. That place is as bad as the school store. No one knows how to do retail up here."

"The gift shop was lovely, I thought." They had stopped in the center of the little town before reaching The Country Store. "This parking lot is impossible."

Margaret found herself having to turn right to go around the block. It was a full half-mile before she found another right turn and then it was a one-way street. Finally, they were headed back toward the summer school. Margaret began to relax.

"Now, tell me," she said, "What would you do differently?"

♫

## Then ~ Year 13

"They hired Penny Corbett." Chris hung her coat on the hook by the kitchen door.

"I thought maybe you'd like it, Chrissy." He kept his eyes on his book to hide his disappointment. To hide his anger.

"We could use the extra money, for sure. But who would look after Stephanie? I can't leave her. She's only nine. If money was that important, you'd do something about it."

Chris pulled a bright box out of her shopping bag. "The Barbies were on sale. I got this for her birthday."

"My mother could keep her. She's home all summer." How many times had he given that answer to the same old objection?

"Well, she shouldn't be. She should get a life."

"Chris, she has one. Mom has her work. She supports herself."

"Better than you do. And she takes better care of herself, too. Look at you, Will. You're putting on weight. Why aren't you running any more?"

"It wasn't doing me any good."

"That's crazy. Will, what is going on?"

"You could ask someone to watch Steffi. Her friend Melody's mom?"

"You could ask Mr. Herman for a raise."

No way was he going to talk about that.

♫

## Then ~ Year 14

The lake was silver blue. Alex was digging a trench in the muddy sand. One-year-old Alyssa was safely in her portable playpen.

Julia sat beside her brother-in-law. No one else in the family was down on the rocks today.

"Jacqueline du Pré," Julia said. "The cellist. She had multiple sclerosis." She shaded her eyes to watch her son. Jacqueline du Pré had been young too, so young.

"But you're the musician," Malcolm said bitterly, then, "Julie, I'm sorry. I didn't mean what that sounded like."

"Twenty years," Julia said. "MS can take twenty years. Maybe more. Maybe a lot more by then." Already, her sister had to stay at home, out of the heat, to protect herself against the symptoms of the disease. I'll bring her down here this evening, Julia thought.

"I'm not going to walk away from the mother of my child."

"I know that, Mal." She didn't know. Nobody could. But her brother-in-law was a decent man. "Money," she said.

"We're managing, Julie."

Yes, she thought, they were managing. But she'd seen the fear behind Cathy's brave eyes, and she'd held her mother in her arms while Elinor cried.

Now she said, "I want more for my sister and you

69

than managing, Mal. Whatever makes your life easier now."

He skipped a stone viciously into the lake.

"What I'm going to do is make a gift, a trust account in Hillport. You won't have to ask. Withdraw what you like. Pretend it was the lottery." She put up her hand. "Don't argue. Philip's ghost would get mad."

"Ah, Julie."

She blinked her eyes hard and fast. "We'll build a new house. You live so close, and Cathy loves Greenlea." She nodded toward the old house on the hill across the swimming bay. "There's no way to make it work for a wheelchair. We'll start over."

"You don't mess around, do you?" her brother-in-law said bitterly.

"I'll buy Cathy whatever I can," Julia said. She sucked in a long breath. "I only wish I could buy a cure."

♫

## Then ~ Year 14

The headlights streamed out in front of the pickup truck. Beyond the expressway, the silhouettes of the mountains had disappeared in the night. There was silence in the dark of the cab. Finally, Chrissy spoke.

"We could try another counselor. Or you could go to one by yourself. Or maybe just to a doctor."

"Chris, I'm okay."

"Will Ehrendorf, you are not! You were never like this, not even in junior high. Even five years ago, you were fine. Then, boom, like a beach ball. Why are you doing this, Will?"

"I'm not doing anything."

"Okay, you're not. Not thinking about all the junk that you eat, not getting any exercise. You're killing yourself."

"No, I'm not."

"You are, and it's stupid, Will. It's awful. You're going to get sick. You're going to have a heart attack."

She was silent a moment, but then she started up again.

"And it's not like it's any accident, like poor Cathy Levan getting MS. That is so sad, and it's so hard on her family. You can tell when you see them. And what about her husband and the baby? What about me and Stephanie? If something happens to you, Will, what about me and Stephanie?"

"Nothing's going to happen to me. If it did, I have insurance."

"Yeah, that you have to pay for yourself, 'cause you won't get a decent job. You know what, Will?"

"What, Chris?"

"You don't care about me."

He took his hand off the wheel and reached over and squeezed her leg. "Oh, come on, Chrissy, you know I do."

And that was the truth. Just not all of it.

♫

## Then ~ Year 15

"My mother has a dulcimer," Jonathan said to Alex.

"Don't touch it," Alex replied.

"Come on, everyone," Emilia said, shooing the boys out of the practice room. "Time for snack."

Julia watched the four boys jostle each other down the apartment hall toward the big kitchen. She closed the door behind them and reached for her violin.

That afternoon, when Justina DaCosta arrived to pick up her son, as usual the last of the parents to arrive, Jonathan informed his mother that "Alex has a dulcimer too."

"My mom does," Alex insisted.

"But aren't you a violinist?" Justina asked Julia.

"And aren't you a lawyer? And a musician, on the side?"

"Actually, yes," Justina said. "Percussion. It put me through school."

"You didn't play hammer dulcimer."

"You got that right." Justina laughed. "I heard one at a folk festival, though. I thought it was gorgeous." She stood in Julia's hallway, elegantly professional from her close-cropped hair to the big silver earrings, through the perfect black suit and slim briefcase, right down to the brand-new white running shoes.

"I'd just finished the bar exam. I had a job and money at last. I got one and taught myself. But there's

73

only so much Celtic mountain music I can take. Why do you have one? Do you play?"

Julia said with a wave of her hand, "It came to me, on Dulcimer Hill." That was what she had called it in her mind since that long-ago day.

She went on, "I keep thinking, there's stuff out there. Violin and whatever. Piano, harp, guitar. Transcribe it for dulcimer and try it."

"Whatever and flute. Debussy wrote a lot of that," Justina said.

Julia looked at her. "Satie." This was cool.

Justina shrugged and grinned. "Pachelbel's greatest hit. Although it's a marathon for the percussion. And actually, it might not work."

"Are you for real? Want to give it a try?"

"Are you busy Sunday, after church?" Justina asked.

"I'll call it my afternoon practice."

"Should I bring this 'un?" Justina asked. Her son was hitching up his backpack.

"Alex will be in Connecticut. Philip's parents are here for a month."

"No prob," Justina said. She looked down at her son. "Aunt Tierra's house for you, young man."

"My cousin has a Doctor Who voice-changing mask," Jonathan informed Alex. Both mothers rolled their eyes.

♬

## Then ~ Year 17

"I went up there with Penny. She showed me around. That house is unbelievable."

He closed the textbook. "Must be, what Randy told us it cost."

"Pen said they had to do it."

"Yeah, sure."

"Well, they did," Chris said. "There was no way the old place would work for Cathy. She can't walk by herself any more. She's, like, in a wheelchair all the time. Her room's on the first floor. The doors are real wide, and there's no bumps or anything. It must be nice to have a rich sister."

Or any sister at all, he thought.

Steffi was at the kitchen table, writing a story. It was this week's second-grade homework.

"Mrs. Warren's not going back," Chris said. "For sure she's way too old by now. Penny's going to be in charge. Cathy's gotten much worse. It makes a lot of work for Pen. She asked if I would come and help."

"Yeah? What'd you tell her?"

"I told her I'd think about it. You going to dry these dishes or what?"

Will levered himself to the front of the couch and pushed himself up. "They'd dry by themselves if you'd use hotter water."

"You saw how much gas we used last month. And

then you go and buy those CDs. It's not even Christian music, Will. Did you talk to Mr. Herman?"

"He's busy." That much was true.

A long silence followed. Chris emptied the dishpan. Will hung up the towel, put away the stack of plates and sorted the utensils into the kitchen drawer.

Chris sighed. "Okay," she said. "I'll take the job. Cleaning that house, at least I'll get paid."

"Whatever," Will said. He worked hard to keep his face expressionless.

# CHAPTER SIX

### Now ~ Year 3

"There's all this stock she ordered," Susanna said. "Pussy hats! They are so over. At least these aren't pink. And we did really well with custom orders last year. She wants the students to work in the store," the fifteen-year-old said disgustedly.

Margaret nodded. "Work-study. It's really not a bad idea."

Susanna said, "Umph," and plopped herself on the couch in Margaret and Henry's cabin. "She stole my store. And kicked you out of your office."

"Ms. Maxwell needs an office. She's here full-time to consult."

"She's running the place. How come you're not pissed off?"

"Because there's not a lot of point," Margaret replied. It was true, Kenneth Anderson's new employee was more than a little controlling. Margaret, however, was able to appreciate Lisa Maxwell's youth and energy and organizing ability, more than Kellie and Susanna did. And another factor gave her perspective. "I've decided to retire at the end of next year."

"Good for you," Susanna said. "Me, I'm unemployed. Again."

♫

## Then ~ Year 17

Will heard the noisy pickup pull up next to the house. The brakes protested. The truck's doors slammed, first Stephanie on the passenger side, then Chris.

Steffi and Chris came into the trailer with bags, excess produce from the big kitchen garden at Greenlea. It was charity. That bothered him. But Chris saw the generosity, or thought of it as extra pay.

Chris liked working for Elinor Fletcher and Julia Levan. Penny directed the housework. Chris helped. And now she helped with Cathy, too, learning from the visiting nurse and the home health aide.

"How was your day?" he asked at the dinner table. He tried to make a point of getting her to talk about what she did up at Greenlea. She was proud of her work, he could tell. He hoped she was getting used to her new feelings of accomplishment, of confidence and competence.

"They don't know why it's going so fast. Sometimes I guess it happens that way, if you get the disease when you're young."

He helped himself to a third biscuit and a second potato.

Chris said, "They asked if I could live with them this winter, Will. Across the lake."

"What did you tell them?"

78

Chrissy looked at him, her pale eyes on him, the first time she had looked at him directly in a very long time.

"I prayed on it. Then I told them yes."

"But, Mom," nine-year-old Stephanie said, "where are Dad and I going to live?"

Chris sighed. "You'll come with me. I asked. You'll have a room of your own."

"But I come back here when school starts, right?"

Chris said, "You'll go to school over there." She turned to Will. "Professor Fletcher says it's a good district. Alyssa's going to Pre-K at the same school where Steff will go."

"And you'll be doing housework? Is Penny going?"

"Of course not," Chris said. "She's got her family. You know she only works in the summer, when they've opened Greenlea."

"You'll do all the housework there?" Dumb question. It could make her change her mind.

"I won't do much housework at all," Chris replied. "They've already got some lady for that. I'll be helping take care of Cathy." She stood to clear the plates from the table.

"What's for dessert?" Will asked.

79

♫

## Then ~ Year 17

"That's it, the brick house," Chrissy said.

Will pulled the pickup into the long drive. Between them, Steffi leaned forward and peered up the hill at the big brick house with white shutters and dormers in the roof. There was movement at one of the windows on the ground floor. The truck ground its way up the drive. Will braked to a stop just as a small figure came racing around from the back of the house.

"Steffi!" Alyssa cried. "Steffi! You're here!"

Chris opened the door and stepped down from her seat, with Stephanie sliding after her.

"Come on," Alyssa commanded to Steffi. "Your room's way up at the top. Look, that's the window," the five-year-old said, pointing up at the dormer that looked out over the city of Hillport toward the lake. "Your room is right over mine. You can tap on the floor to send me a message. I'll show you." Alyssa, with red curls like her mother's, tugged at Stephanie's arm.

"Go on," Chris said to her daughter. "Go see your princess bed." As the girls ran off toward the house, Chris looked guiltily at Will.

Elinor Fletcher and Malcolm Tennant came toward the truck. Malcolm looked in the back, then grinned at Chris.

"That's not so much," he said, nodding at the half-dozen cardboard boxes.

Will lowered himself carefully from the driver's seat and lumbered back to the side of the truck. "These are going up to the top?" He frowned.

"Not a problem," Malcolm said with an easy smile. "We've got some young legs. Alex, Jon," he called toward the back yard. "Come lend us a hand."

Nine-year-old Alex came around the house with a dark boy of the same age. "What's up?" Alex asked.

"Steffi and Chris are moving in. Can you chaps help me get these cartons upstairs?"

Elinor spoke. "Christine, we're so glad to see you. And Will. Come out to the garden and have some tea."

The back garden of the big house was brimming with color in the late June sun. Will looked at the chairs arrayed on the porch and decided the wooden bench looked sturdy enough. He lowered himself onto it.

"It's beautiful," he said to Professor Fletcher. He remembered that when he was a kid and saw her around the village, her hair had been a real dark red, like Cathy's and Alyssa's. It was gray now. He reckoned there was enough reason.

"It means a lot to Cathy," she said. "She can see it from inside. We've had to move her downstairs."

"I'm sorry," Will said. The double doors began to open. Chris moved to hold the doors. Malcolm Tennant backed through them, pulling his wife's wheelchair backward. Chris closed the doors. Will thought, They've done that a lot.

Will had not seen Cathy for nearly four years. There were padded wings on the wheelchair now, for when she

81

couldn't hold up her head. Chris said Cathy only had one or two good hours at a time, and then she got tired and couldn't speak clearly and could hardly control her hands or her head. Sometimes she just cried. Now must be one of the good times. Cathy's red curls nodded in the early August sun. Her round face was eager and open, the way he remembered when she'd come to play with Sharon. She had trained to be a teacher, in primary grades just like his mom. Cathy would have been good at that. It was, he thought, a rotten shame.

Alyssa burst through the door. "Dad, can we go down to the club? Steffi said she'd go with us."

"Sure, baby. Go ahead. Be back in time for dinner."

Chris said, "Alyssa, Steff has to be home at six. We're going shopping for school clothes. Remind her, will you, please?"

"Yeah, sure." Alyssa was gone, the screen door slamming behind her.

Chris stood up. She picked up the empty pitcher of tea. "I'll make some more." She went into the house. And Julie came out. She was followed by a tall black woman with close-cropped hair, wearing long leggings, a colorful tunic top, and a whole lot of large gold jewelry. Her bracelets piled up nearly to her elbows.

Cathy turned her head toward Will. "I can't tell you how grateful we are. For Steffi being so good with Lys, and everything that Chris does for me. I don't know..."

Cathy's face clouded over and tears filled her eyes. Julia bent toward her sister. Elinor and Malcolm both nodded toward Will in agreement.

Elinor said, "Christine is a miracle. She's been so

82

generous with her time and her patience. You have a wonderful family, Will."

Yeah, he thought, I do. It's just not the one I wanted. He looked at the black woman with Julie. He wondered who Julie's family was now.

What he said was, "It's good for us too, Chrissy finding something she wants to do." What he didn't say was that Chris could go on doing it, long after this was over. And find a life of her own, for herself. Without him. He hoped without him.

♫

Julia watched Will Ehrendorf pull himself up and maneuver into the driver's seat. She hoped her thoughts didn't show, but Chrissy's flushed, embarrassed face told her they had.

The pickup sputtered to life. He got it turned around in the drive. They watched in silence as it rolled down the drive, listing leftward, trailing a cloud of burned oil.

Malcolm spoke. "Now," he said, smiling down at Stephanie, "what about this shopping trip? The lass'll be wanting her finery. Which car shall Christine take?"

"Car?" Chrissy said.

"You'll need a car," Elinor said. "We thought Cathy's. And Malcolm will show you how the lift van works, the locks for the chair. It's really quite easy. I've done it myself."

Julia turned away toward the house. She walked up

the slope thinking, I've got to get rid of that dulcimer.

Beside her, Justina hummed the word, "Large."

"What?"

"Large. He's large," Tina hummed. "Remember Popeye? Olive Oyl and Bluto? He's large."

Julia laughed.

"How does she stand it, do you suppose?" Justina asked.

"She doesn't. That's why she's here."

"Ah. I see. What did she ever see in him?"

"He wasn't always like that," Julia said.

♪

## Then ~ Year 19

"Julie," her sister said. Cathy's body trembled; her feet stuttered across the floor. Julia put her arm across her sister's thin back and tightened her grip on Cathy's arm. They reached the waiting wheelchair. Julie eased Cathy into the chair, fastened the strap across her lap, and lifted her sister's feet to the footrests. Cathy's head shook between the rests, her curly red hair duller than it used to be but still a contrast against the black padding.

"Julie," Cathy said again. Her voice was clear and strong today. "You have to promise me."

Julia sat in the lift chair next to her sister's bed. She leaned forward and took both of Cathy's hands in her own.

"I can't."

"You have to. You're the strongest. And you can defend yourself."

"What I can't do, Cathy, is give up hope. We won't give up."

"I have. I've given up hope."

"Not yet! You don't mean now."

"No, not yet. But when it gets too much, when there's nothing left, when I can't be at home."

"You'll always be able to be at home. We have Chris. We can get a professional nurse."

Cathy tightened her grip on Julia's hands. "Promise me, Julie. I'll find a way to let you know when it's time."

85

Julia closed her eyes. "Maybe," she said. "I can't make a promise now." She looked at her sister. "Maybe it won't be that bad."

"Maybe not," Cathy agreed. "But I want to be peaceful, Julie. I just want to fall asleep. I want that to be what Lyssa remembers."

Julia felt tears filling her eyes. "Oh, Cathy," she whispered.

♫

"Caring for the MS Patient." Julia read the cover of the brochure aloud.

"The MS Society sent me all these. I was wondering..." Christine's voice trailed off.

"Wondering what?" Julia asked encouragingly. It always amazed her, how unsure Chris was of her place in the world.

"There's a class over here we found out about. It's called 'Home Health Skills for Caregivers.' Look, I printed it out."

Julia read the course description from the Hillport Community College. "And?"

"Well," Chris said, "I wasn't good at school, but..."

"But you graduated."

"Yes." Chrissy's face had gotten red.

"You could do this. Is that what you mean?"

"But it's two nights a week."

86

"What nights will my mother and Malcolm teach this term? As long as one of them is home. And Steffi can be here, can't she? She's good with Cathy, almost as good as you are."

"You mean, I could? It would be okay?"

"Anything you can learn will help. It's only going to get harder, God knows."

"I pray on it every day. I put her on the prayer list at church."

Julia tried to smile. The world of church and prayer lists was far from her own. She felt as uncomfortable with Chrissy's praying as Chrissy would feel on a concert stage. "It doesn't always help, you know," she said gently.

"Not so we can see right now. That's what Reverend Tom says. That's how it was when his wife died of cancer. But he thinks the praying eased her mind. It eased his, for sure. He told me so."

"Your new church is very important to you." The small white building was two miles away. Chris had pointed it out to Cathy as Julia drove to the ferry last fall. Their long-time housekeeper belonged to the church. She had invited Chris to go with her to services.

"It is," Chris agreed. "It's wonderful. Someplace that takes me in, that doesn't care what Uncle Art and Aunt Marian think or blame me for being a burden to Grandma. Someplace that forgives mistakes. That's important to me."

Good Lord, Julia thought. And wondered if maybe that was a prayer.

♫

"Lose the weight," Dr. Moriseau said to Will. "You're on borrowed time as it is. Look, go see this gal, Peg McGehee. She's a dietitian. Can your wife go with you? If you're going to see forty, you've got to make a lifestyle change."

"We're separated," Will said. "She's living here in Hillport."

"Ah," Dr. Moriseau said, rubbing the top of his balding head. "She take the kids? How many you got?"

"Just the one, Steff. Yeah, she's with Chris. She's gonna go to school there."

"So you're shopping and cooking for yourself. That could be good, or it could be bad. I remember when my first wife left. You've got no margin for error, Will. You can't take any chances. You go see Peg."

The same thing that Marnie, his friend from the music store, now said. "I know you've been unhappy, Will. But it's time you start taking care of yourself."

Her husband Rob came in from their barbecue with the plate of burgers, calling their two little boys to get out of the wading pool.

"So, man," he said, peering through the glasses that had changed from round to rectangular over the years, "where're we at on the reading list?"

"I'm done with the Chinese history," Will said. He pulled a folded sheet of paper out of his pocket. "Next is Japan. I hope the names are easier to remember."

"They're not," Rob said. "One damn dynasty after

88

another. Come on, guys," he called to his sons. "Let's eat. Will and I have to go to the library."

# CHAPTER SEVEN

### Now ~ Year 4

The beam of Margaret's flashlight streamed ahead of her and touched a graveled berm. The road, at last. With that thought, she admitted how alarmed she had been.

Toward her left, the road sloped downhill. She walked that way. After only a few minutes, she began to make out the faint sound of music in the distance. Lights became visible up ahead. Soon, she would reach the drive.

"Margaret? Is that you? Margaret?"

"Susanna? What are you doing way out here?"

"Omigod, Margaret. We were so worried. Where have you been? Henry said you went for a walk."

"Yes," Margaret said. "I didn't mean to make you upset."

Will Ehrendorf's large body emerged from the shadows beside the drive.

"You're all right, then," he said. Margaret was, as always, intrigued by the surprisingly light tenor voice in such a large man. But then, she thought, he wasn't meant to be so big.

"Did Henry send you out to find me?"

"No," Susanna said. "He's not worried. Except about

90

the microphones."

"Um," Margaret said noncommittally.

"So, why'd you go and disappear?" Susanna demanded. "You could at least have told somebody where you were."

"I did tell Henry," Margaret observed. "It's sweet of you to be concerned." She gave Susanna's shoulders a squeeze.

"Yeah, but why?" Susanna asked. "You were in with him, Dr. Anderson. I know. Kellie told me."

"It's been a rather difficult day."

"That bad," Will said. "Difficult."

"He fired me," Margaret said. "At the end of the season. I couldn't tell Henry. He's fired us both." As the words and the fact emerged into the evening air, she felt filled with relief.

"Dickhead."

"Susanna!"

"Well, Margaret, he is." The girl bent, picked up a stone, and hurled it into the woods.

"I haven't looked for a job in twenty years." Margaret sighed. "My Social Security depends on these years. And Aubrey, our daughter, is moving to Albany. I was so looking forward to next summer here."

"And who's gonna take over for you?" Susanna wanted to know.

"Ms. Maxwell will be running the office. I'm to orient her," Margaret said with distaste.

"I bet he said 'orien*tate*,' didn't he, Margaret? I can

tell from your voice."

"Susanna, you know me far too well."

They were approaching the performance shed. It was intermission; most of the audience was out on the lawn.

"Anyway," Will Ehrendorf said, "can you and Henry come over for dinner tomorrow? You, too," he said to Susanna.

"Oh," Margaret said. She glanced at Susanna, who raised her eyebrows but nodded.

"My mom said to invite you at seven. Does that sound right?" Will asked.

"Perfect," said Margaret. "Very convenient."

"I want to do it the proper way. But don't worry, mom's going to cook. My daughter will help."

"Will your wife be there?" Susanna asked.

The overhead lights in the shed blinked off and on. It was time to find seats. They moved with the crowd towards the door.

"No," Will said. "She filed for divorce last week."

♫

## Then ~ Year 25

"That's for you," Christine said. She pushed the pieces of paper across the dining table.

He unfolded the paper. There it was, after all these years. Two sheets, stapled together. A date, rubber stamped just yesterday, and a line where the judge had signed. It didn't look that important.

"Where's Steff?"

"She said she didn't want to come. She doesn't want a lot these days. I guess that goes with being fifteen. She doesn't want to live with me and Tom after we get married. She doesn't want to leave her friends. She doesn't want to live with you."

"She told me." He suspected it was the trailer, in its run-down, unrepaired, messy condition, that was keeping Stephanie away.

Chris broke the silence. "She loves you, Will. You're the only father she's ever known."

Their eyes met. "What is that supposed to mean?"

Her glance slid away. "You embarrass her."

"Chris."

"Well, you do."

"You did the best you could, Christine."

"Yes," she said. "I guess I did."

♫

He pulled the colorful, slim and shiny brochure out from between the cracker boxes shelved in the kitchen. He'd found the brochure at the library in Cumberland. He'd forgotten about the music school. Since the laundromat had closed and moved to Allison, music people didn't come to the village any more.

The school had concerts two times a week, on Wednesdays and Sundays, sometimes the teachers, mostly the students.

Wednesdays were his afternoon off. The store closed early on Sundays, at five.

The concerts were free.

♫

### Then ~ Year 25

Julia sat on the far edge of the bed, beside the window that overlooked the sky-blue lake and the garden. The early spring flowers had begun to bloom. Janet Hagedorn, Cathy's doctor, stood on the other side of the bed, next to Malcolm in his usual chair.

"It's time for hospice," Janet said gently.

Julia held her sleeping sister's hand.

"I promised her, no nursing homes."

"What else did you promise her?" Janet asked.

"She wants to fall asleep."

"She will," Janet said.

"Soon?" Malcolm asked. "Look how hard it's gotten for her to breathe. She's exhausted." He smoothed the red curls back from her forehead.

Cathy opened her eyes. She struggled to speak. Her gaze turned from her husband and clung to Julie.

"Soon," Janet said.

♫

His mother went to Cathy's funeral in Hillport. It was Wednesday. He could have gone, even though Mike Herman needed him now since Joey was still in school. Instead, he had come here to his sister's grave. Mary Fran came here twice a year, on Memorial Day and on

Sharon's birthday. Will visited alone all the other times. For himself, he knew. He came to this hillside with flowers for Sharon, to touch the stone and take away strength.

On his afternoon off, and no one at home, he had walked to the cemetery today, a mile from home, at a ponderous pace. He could start getting more exercise now. The divorce had been final for over a year. Christine had married the widower who pastored her church in Vermont. No matter what happened to Chris, he was free. He could go back to being the way he was. If he could. If it wasn't too late.

He remembered Julie's face, that day in Hillport. But she still had the dulcimer he had given her. The black woman played it, Stephanie said, and Julie played the violin. And Steffi said they both loved Julie.

"Who does?" he'd asked.

The black lady, Tina. And Malcolm Tennant, Julie's brother-in-law, and now that Cathy had died, they would see.

He had made an appointment next week with the dietitian. It might be too late.

♫

Julia looked at Malcolm's fine-boned face, the dusting of faint English freckles under the pale blue eyes. "No, Mal," she said firmly. "It's just not there."

Her brother-in-law dropped his hands from her shoulders. He made a rueful face and turned toward the

96

door of the living room. "Oh, well."

"I'm sorry," she said.

He stopped. "Your mother, you know, she worries about your being alone."

"Gallant Mal steps into the breach?"

"Indeed, throwing myself at your feet."

"Your cape will do, but no," Julie said with a smile. She turned back toward the window overlooking the lake and watched Malcolm's reflection as he left the room. She was very glad to be alone. She was tired, bone tired.

Outside, rain was falling steadily. A silver mist hung over the lake. Somewhere on the other side was Greenlea, the summer house, in its high meadow, gazing back. And she wasn't there. This was the first time in more years than she could recall that she hadn't been in the house at Greenlea in August. But this was another year of sadness. The sad years were different. They should be different.

There were so many losses. It felt good to be alone. Alone meant no one would disappear from her life. She would take Alex to school next week. These two weeks were precious each year. Her son was growing up and growing away.

There was a chill in the room. She hugged herself. There were times she remembered from years ago, the warmth of those afternoons on Dulcimer Hill. How sweet and foolish that had been. She could still send the dulcimer back. She should box it up and have it delivered. That was simple and obvious. She could have done it years ago. She should have done it years ago. She

97

pictured him opening the box, the grotesquely fat man across the lake. What would it matter? He wouldn't care. Too many years had passed for that.

# CHAPTER EIGHT

### Now ~ Year 4

"Yo, Will," Susanna said. "Lookin' good." She stopped in the aisle of the performance hall, stepped backward, and looked him over. "Bulking down, huh?"

She's right, Margaret thought. They took their seats for the last concert of the year. The last concert of her last year in the mountains, near the lake. The August evening was cool.

Later, during the intermission, before Will came back to his seat, Susanna and Margaret were sitting alone. "You think he's getting cuter?" Susanna asked.

Margaret considered the question and eventually she nodded. "He's not an unattractive man, although, I must say, those overalls..."

Susanna said, "He's still got a long way to go. My grandpa used to say, 'Cherchez la femme.' I wonder who it is? Probably someone I couldn't stand. I'm sixteen now," she added.

Margaret looked at Susanna solemnly, but she felt her mouth twitching. "And I'm sixty-two and married. That's terrible timing for both of us, assuming you're right, that our country friend could become a bit of a heart-breaker."

"Our country friend. That's good, Margaret, that's very good."

99

♫

## Then ~ Year 25

The telephone rang through the empty store. Mike was up front; he would answer. Will bent over the cases of canned goods. The phone rang again. It would be Angie Herman, telling Mike it was time to come home. Will heard Mike grunt, on his way to the phone, then the sound of something, a cardboard end-aisle display, the sound it made when a customer knocked it over, and a heavier thud.

The phone rang again. Mike would answer. Meanwhile, Will could restack the cereal boxes. The telephone rang a fourth time.

Will brushed through the curtain into the front of the store. The boxes were scattered across the floor. Mike was lying there on his back, his face as white and pasty as bread, beads of sweat breaking out.

"Mike, Jesus," Will said. He bent, then straightened and reached the counter and grabbed the receiver off the hook. "Angie?"

"Where's Michael?"

"He's sick. Angie, call an ambulance. It might be his heart."

"He's sick? I told him..."

"Angie, get help. Call the ambulance. Now." He hung up the phone. He went over and squatted beside Mike Herman. "It's okay, man. It'll be okay."

♫

It wasn't okay. He left the hospital at five in the morning, leaving Angie with her son Greg, his wife and their kids. He went to the store and dealt with the waiting distributor's truck and pulled the shades. He neatly lettered "CLOSED" on a piece of white cardboard and taped it up to the door.

Then he went home and had more coffee and breakfast and showered and shaved. At nine o'clock, in his only suit that was getting too big, he walked into the bank and asked to talk to Eileen Magedsen, the manager in charge. After he left the bank, he drove by the store. Already, a bouquet of flowers lay on the front step. People did that, nowadays.

Joanne sang at the funeral. Afterwards, beside the grave on a glorious autumn day, she stood beside him. Elinor Fletcher was there with her mother, the ancient Alice Fletcher. They didn't come to the Hermans' house. Joanne did. His mother did, looking worn and pale. And so, too, did Chris, and her husband the Reverend Tom, and Stephanie.

Chris said, "We need to talk to you, Will. About Stephanie. We'll come by the house after dinner."

♫

"It's not much," Will said. "Sixty thousand dollars." The Reverend Tom's eyebrows rose. "It was more, before. The market went down," he said to Chris.

101

"Where did you get it, Will?" she asked.

"I didn't touch my dad's insurance. My friend Marnie invested it. She feels pretty bad that it's not as much as it used to be."

"It's enough," said the Reverend Tom. He squeezed Steffi's shoulder. She pulled away. She was slumped in one of his mother's kitchen chairs, staring at Will.

"You never told me," Christine said to Will. "We could have used it to buy a house."

"We didn't need to buy a house."

"It's not enough," Stephanie said. "I want to go to away to school. That costs more."

"Honey, it's not a good idea," Chris said. "You being the first in the family and all."

"I'm not the first. Grandma went to Cumberland. That was far away for her."

Yeah, Will thought, and she went to a bar with her friends and she met my dad. Lucky her.

They heard a car pull up outside the house. Will hauled himself up and went to the door. Joanne was there.

"I'm not interrupting, am I?" She pushed past him into the dining room. "Everybody thinks I know." She smiled brightly at all of them. "What's going to happen to the store?"

♫

"It's my belief that people with bad attitudes have them for damn good reasons," Julia said to Stephanie. They were sitting across from each other at the island counter in the big kitchen in Hillport. They each had a tall glass of cider. The burnt orange cider echoed the leaves of the tall oak tree outside. The fragrance of baking bread escaped from the oven.

"It's not that they aren't nice, Tom and Joanne," Stephanie said. "I mean, Joanne, she said to me she's gonna wait to marry my dad until Christmas a year from now. So it won't interfere with my graduation and me getting ready for college. But they try too hard to be good to me, Joanne and Tom, you know what I mean?"

"I know what you mean. I tried too hard with the clan Kavadas. They despised me for it. At least that's how it felt."

"Alex says..."

"Yes?"

Stephanie sucked in a breath. "He says he's not a natural child. But he is a Kavadas."

"Did he tell you why that was?"

"So you and Alex wouldn't get AIDS."

"How did he happen to tell you that?"

"Oh, you know, we talk about stuff. We were up on the hill. We were talking about our families."

"The hill?"

"Y'know, the hill behind your house."

"Yes," Julia said. "That's a good place to talk about families." She thought it would take her some time to get used to Alex and Stephanie meeting up on Dulcimer Hill.

They sat in silence for a while. Finally, Stephanie

said, "Julie? Why did you tell him?"

Julia sighed. "Because I thought he'd find out anyway. A music critic told me he's planning to write Philip's biography. He's picked up the rumor about Phil, about Philip and my dad. He intends to publish that. It will sell a lot of books."

"But it's been a secret for such a long time," Stephanie said.

"Philip's family wants it that way."

"I guess it's the same way my family does." Stephanie ran her finger around her glass. "They don't think anyone needs to know. Anyone means me."

Julia frowned. "Know what? I don't understand."

"Last year, with my birthday money, I wanted to get one of those DNA analyses," Stephanie said. "Well, not just one. Mom and Dad's too. They both said no."

Julia looked at the girl. "Why? I mean, why did you want DNA from them?"

Stephanie sat up straight. "Well, not from Dad. That's pretty obvious. But Mom. Her mother disappeared, you know. Ran off and left my mom behind. She called home from Albany. They never heard from her again. She never said who my mother's father was. There might have been a match, you know?"

Julia though of her own mother's family. The Fletchers could trace their roots back several hundred years. That didn't mean much, but it did put life in perspective. It gave them an interest in history, a feeling of knowing someone who'd been present at or near historic events. The family tree had led Julia's mother

104

Elinor to become an historian.

"I wonder why," she said to Stephanie now. "Even if there's a black sheep or some scoundrel, if it's in the past, it's interesting."

"I don't think it's that," Stephanie said. "I got the feeling it's something about me. About them."

"An illness? A risky gene? You'd think they'd want to know, would want you to know."

"That's probably what it is," Stephanie said. "Mom, she doesn't like doctors. She doesn't like hospitals. She always thinks praying will make things all better. She thinks you did the right thing, keeping Cathy at home."

"We had a lot of professional help," Julia observed.

# CHAPTER NINE

## Now and Then

"Kellie said we can stay at her house. No motel."

"That's such an imposition, Susanna." Margaret shifted the phone against her ear.

"But that's what friends are *for*, Margaret. Poor Will, I bet he's bummed about his mom. Even though she was old."

"She was my age," Margaret said quietly.

"Anyway," Susanna said, "I can get on the train in Poughkeepsie. I'll look for you, okay?"

"That will be fine. I'll see you tomorrow, then, at eleven."

Margaret hung up the phone and sighed. Poor Mary Fran Ehrendorf, such a pleasant woman, dead in her sleep before she'd even begun the retirement in Florida she'd talked about at dinner last year.

The next day, there was Susanna, in jeans and a hooded sweatshirt, bouncing in her running shoes on the Poughkeepsie platform. And there was Kellie at the station in Malburg Bay, in a parka and boots. Snow still lay on the ground, and a cold wind blew through the bleak spring day.

"Jase and the kids went up to Cumberland," Kellie told them. "On the way back, he's dropping them off

106

with Joanne's neighbor. She's keeping them all. They'll spend the night with their cousins. They cleaned up their rooms real neat for you two."

"Joanne? The one you said is marrying Will?" Susanna asked.

"Did I tell you that?"

"In your Christmas card," Susanna said.

"I'm not so sure anymore," Kellie said. "It's her idea and not his. He's kinda busy, getting ready to build his store."

"Good heavens," Margaret said. "He's building a store of his own? He told me once he wanted to travel."

"You own a store, you don't leave it for long," Susanna said. "Unless you have really trustworthy help."

♫

"Mom?"

Her son's voice at the door yanked Julia's attention away from her packing.

"Sweetie, what's up?" She still was surprised to have to look up at her handsome Greek son.

He stepped into the room. "Stephanie's grandmother died."

"Oh, Alex." She hugged him. "What happened? When?"

"They think she had a stroke. Will found her yesterday in her bed. He came over to tell Steff. She's pretty messed up. She went home with her dad. She

107

called me from there."

Justina stuck her head around the door. "You ready?"

Julie held up her hand. "Did Steffi know when the funeral will be?" she asked Alex. Tina came in and sat down on the bed.

"Day after tomorrow. Can I go up? I'll have to miss school a couple of days." His voice sounded deeper than yesterday, and he must have grown another inch.

"Of course," Julie said. "Oh, Alex, I'm glad you can go. I can't cancel Paris."

The telephone rang.

"Julie, dear?" Her mother sounded older, too.

"Hi, Mom. It's terrible news, about Mary Fran." She put her hand over the phone and said to Tina, "Steffi's grandmother died."

"And unnerving," Elinor said on the phone. "She was three years younger than I."

"Are you doing flowers?"

"Of course. Shall I include you?"

"Please," Julie said.

"Me, too," Tina mouthed and gestured.

"I tell you what," Julia said to her mother. "Do something separate for me, if you would, and put Tina on it too. Poor Steffi. Will Chris and Tom be there, do you think?"

"I would hope Chris will be there," Elinor said, "for Stephanie's sake. And her own. It seems like the end of an era, somehow."

"Yes," her daughter agreed. "You're right, it does."

♫

"Can I stay here tonight?"

Will looked at Stephanie, standing in the trailer door. He pulled the earphones off his head. "Sure, Steff. Of course you can."

She came in and sat on the sagging old couch. "Grandma's house is too lonely. She ought to be there."

Will turned off the CD player. "She ought to be with her friends in Florida."

"You believe those people, wanting to look at the house today?"

"Honey, how would they know?"

"You can keep it now, can't you, Dad? Live there yourself?"

"I don't think so, Steffi," Will said slowly.

"Why not? The steps aren't a problem any more. Just look at you. Like back to normal. You know what, Dad? I should tell you, I really should." She closed her eyes.

"Steffi, what? Is something wrong?"

"I am so glad you lost the weight. I used to think..." She opened her eyes. "I used to be so embarrassed, like at my graduation. But you don't, Dad, and I am so glad. I want you to know."

Will cleared his throat. "Those people might want to buy the house. We could use the money, Steff. We could."

"But, Dad, I got the scholarship."

"I know. That's wonderful. Thing is, Steffi, I'm buying the store."

"From Angie? You're buying the store? That old dump?" She stopped. "I'm sorry, Dad."

"It's a new building, is what it would mean. A better building, with good lights."

"Like the new Gilson's in Cumberland?"

"Better," Will said. "But not that big. And the old building will make something funky. Not food. Used furniture, maybe."

"Vintage," Stephanie said. "Jeez, Daddy. You know what Grandma would say about that? How happy she'd be if you owned a brand-new grocery store? You think we can call those people back?"

Will smiled at his tall daughter, home in the middle of her freshman year at Syracuse, no need to worry about her grades, her black curls bobbing, her eyes sparkling with her own happiness at the news from the only father she'd ever known.

# CHAPTER TEN

### Now

"You know, Margaret," Susanna said slowly.

Margaret was drying the last of Mary Frances Ehrendorf's tableware as Kellie washed. Will and Stephanie were putting the dishes away. And Julia Levan's son was sitting at the kitchen table. If only Kenneth Anderson could know.

"I have this idea," Susanna said.

"Clearly," Margaret observed.

"Uh-oh," Kellie said. "That's how we got the online school store."

"Well, that was a good idea," Susanna said indignantly. "And so's this one. Margaret and Henry can buy this house."

"Oh, I don't think so," Joanne said, bringing more dishes into the kitchen. "It's Will's house now, isn't it, honey?"

Joanne looked sideways up at Will, and Margaret felt a small pang of envy. The fat man was gone – she couldn't quite imagine where – and in his place was a tall and well-made heartbreaker, indeed. She'd been right about that. A shy one, though: the wistful country bumpkin she'd met four, almost five, years ago wasn't entirely gone. He still looked out from under the spill of

111

curly hair. Margaret wondered what the wistfulness was about. She thought it must be more than his mother.

He said now, "Come on, Jo. It is for sale."

"Yeah," Susanna said. "What Margaret's doing these days, the typing for lawyers, she does it over the internet. So, she could do it anywhere, right?"

Susanna looked to Stephanie for agreement, and Stephanie nodded.

"I mean," Susanna said, "if your grandmother's not here, it might as well be a friend of Will's. So Margaret and Henry can be near Aubrey and Richard and their kids down in Albany. And," she said, and waited.

"Oh, my," Margaret said.

"And?" Will prompted. "What's the and?"

"And," Susanna continued, "there's enough rooms. I could stay in one this summer. Margaret can be the chaperone. Then I can work for you in your store!"

"Which store?" Stephanie asked with interest.

"Which store?" Alex wondered. "There's more than one?"

"Both," Susanna said. "Will's gotta keep an eye on the builders. And getting the new one up, trying to run the old one too, that's gonna be a zoo."

Kellie spoke. "Margaret and Henry, live up here? Hey, Margaret, the lawyer over in Allison, Tad Jaczewski, he'll be needing a secretary. Right, Will, when Velma retires?"

"Now, wait a minute," Joanne said.

"Yeah, slow down a minute." Will was laughing. "It's

Margaret's life."

"Not to mention Henry's," Margaret said. "But just offhand, how much was your mother asking, Will?"

The answer stunned her. Less than half the value of her home in Baltimore. Not only possible, it might indeed be a good thing, quite a good thing. The thought must be showing on her face, Margaret guessed, judging by the disappointment on Joanne's.

♫

Alex had said it was all right. Stephanie told Will so when she ducked under the old wire fence that marked the boundary between the Ehrendorf farm and Greenlea. Will looked around as he followed his daughter up the hill. Nothing, of course, would be the same, on the path he'd avoided for eighteen years. Nor was it different. There was the rock outcrop that marked the halfway point.

At the top, Stephanie strode across the glade to the edge of the cliff. She turned to watch Will catch up. "Look! Isn't it gorgeous? I can see my whole life from here. Except you can't see Hillport."

"You can't see Grandma's house," Will pointed out. "And you can't see Syracuse."

Stephanie slowly turned in a circle, looking around her.

"Don't get dizzy," Will said sharply. "Come back from the edge." She did.

"It's like there's no one left," she said.

"There isn't, is there," he agreed.

"It's like I don't even have a home. But I like Henry and Margaret," she added quickly. "I'm glad your friends could buy Grandma's house. But where are you going to live?"

He shrugged.

"With nowhere but that trailer to live. Dad, you gotta do something else. You know, you could always move in with Joanne."

"No," he said. "I don't want to do that."

She scraped the toe of her shoe along the rock. "I wish you could take me back to school. Joanne could help in the store. Susanna can show her what to do."

"I don't want help from Joanne."

Stephanie looked at him curiously. "You'd better tell her that."

"I will. I've let it go on too long."

He looked at the acres of green treetops between the hill and the glistening blue ribbon of lake. The Fletcher houses were down there among those trees.

He didn't want to live with Joanne. That was the truth. Just not all of it.

# CHAPTER ELEVEN

## Now

The screen door clattered. Stephanie Ehrendorf sat down beside Margaret near the back of the hall. Will took the aisle seat next to his daughter. He needed only one seat. Margaret noticed a woman turn to look at him and take her time in turning away. Amazing, what cheekbones and a jawline could do.

Henry had gone backstage, "just to have a word with Don," he'd said. Now he came up the aisle to join their daughter and the grandchildren. And there was Susanna, pulling away from the group of people in front of the stage and making her way back, followed by that awfully nice boy, Alex Kavadas. At the beginning of the summer, when Susanna and Alex had met again at Stephanie's I'm-home-for-the-summer party, Margaret had feared that she might have underestimated the job of being Susanna's chaperone. Susanna assured her that she and Alex were just good friends, liked to hang out, mostly while stocking shelves at Will's new store. Will had promised he'd keep an eye out.

"Where's Kellie?" Susanna asked now.

"In the dining hall, fussing about the reception," Margaret said.

"And where's Mrs. Brent?" Alex asked politely of Will.

115

"Joanne's more a Shania fan."

Stephanie snorted. "Joanne and my dad broke up," she informed the group. "As of last week. Dad's so into classical."

"It's possible to like both," Margaret's son-in-law, Richard, said in his calming way. "Aubrey's a big Shania fan, too."

"Yeah," said nine-year-old Kendra. "We all know 'I Got Better Things to Do' by heart, don't we, Mom?"

"My favorite song," Aubrey said with a grin, "right after the Barber violin concerto."

"Mom's working on that one," Alex said. "It's her touring piece again this year."

"Really?" said Aubrey. "Anywhere near?"

"Boston," said Alex, "in January."

"Boston," Aubrey said dreamily.

Richard raised his eyebrows. "Guess I'd better get that onto my Christmas list."

"Cool," Alex said. He would be going to college in Cambridge. Susanna smiled happily.

The noise in the hall quieted as Kenneth Anderson climbed to the stage. Lisa Maxwell took her seat in the front row, next to their guest. Margaret had little doubt that Lisa Maxwell's energy was good for the music school or that it was Lisa's charm, not Dr. Anderson's, that had brought Julia Levan to their hall tonight. That, and Kellie mentioning to Lisa that Ms. Levan's son would no doubt encourage his mother to present awards to a group that included Susanna Hemelin's brother.

This evening, the two runners-up had their

moments, to hearty applause, and then it was Jordan Kesto's turn. Even Susanna, Margaret saw with amusement, could not help sitting taller, proud of her brother. He finished his piece with a flourish and took his bows.

Now it was time for Julia Levan. Long applause followed Dr. Anderson's introduction as Ms. Levan rose from her seat and climbed to the stage. She was wearing an elegant long black dress. She took each plaque from Dr. Anderson and presented it to the honored students, Jordan last in first place. She spoke a moment to each, eliciting inaudible answers and appropriately bashful smiles. As the students returned to their seats on the stage and Kenneth Anderson to his in the front row, Julia Levan stood tuning her violin, moving around the stage as she did so.

Margaret happened to glance at Will. Did he need reminding that this was an event that might never occur in his life again, the chance to hear such talent? Apparently not, Margaret concluded. He was already watching the stage with intense concentration.

Julia Levan lifted her violin to her chin, and the hall grew quiet. The music began.

♫

"What do you mean?" Susanna demanded of Will. "Of course you're coming with us." She was leaning toward the dining hall, brightly lit for the evening's post-concert reception.

Earlier in the evening, when Julia Levan and her son had arrived with Dr. Anderson, Alex's eyes had searched the hall till he saw Stephanie Ehrendorf. He started toward her. Lisa Maxwell had noticed and followed. Alex made introductions, and Lisa opened her arms and included them all in an invitation to the reception for Ms. Levan.

"I wouldn't fit in," Will said now. Stephanie looked embarrassed.

"Hah," said Susanna. "Last year, you wouldn't fit. Besides, I need a date."

"Susanna," Margaret said, frowning.

"Margaret," Susanna said. She said to Will, "That bunch of teenage twits? You can't imagine how hard a time they used to give me about my friends. All they understand is the surface. So, let 'em see I was right about the surface, too. Come on, Will, please?"

"Yeah, Dad," Stephanie said with a grin. "She needs a date. Alex'll have to make do with me."

Will let Susanna drag him along with the crowd toward the dining hall, and Margaret hurried to keep up. Will suddenly stopped.

"Susanna," he said. He was gripping the girl's upper arm. "Don't wreck it." His eyes were boring into hers. "Not even a joke."

"Yeah, okay," Susanna said. She turned toward the dining hall again. "I hear you. Okay."

Inside the crowded hall, Margaret moved away to make an inspection tour. Everything moved smoothly without her, she saw, despite Kellie's slightly breathless air when Margaret finally found her.

A large group had surrounded Kenneth Anderson, Lisa Maxwell and Julia Levan, the Kesto family among them. People were anxious to speak to the star, to have their moment in the sun.

Margaret craned her neck, looking for Henry's silver hair. Stephanie and Alex had led Margaret's grand-children toward the food, with their parents hovering behind. Henry was at the other end of the hall, talking to Susanna and Will. By the time she reached them, the group had grown larger. All young women, Margaret observed, students not famous for being close to Susanna before. Susanna was airily answering inane questions about her job this summer, a smugly patient expression on her face. Margaret caught Henry's eye. He too appeared amused.

There was a stir behind her, and a woman in a long black dress emerged from the crowd, a violin case under her arm. The girls around Susanna and Will broke apart.

"You're Jordan's sister," Julia Levan said to Susanna. "Hi, Will. I thought that was you."

Will cleared his throat. "Hi, Julie," he managed to say. "This is Susanna."

"Susanna, of course." Julia Levan extended her hand.

"And my friends," Will said, his voice growing more confident. "Margaret and Henry Renfrew. They bought our house." Julia gave them a dazzling smile. Suddenly, Margaret realized, the schoolgirls were out of the circle and she and Henry were in.

"Julie's kind of a neighbor of ours," Will explained to

119

the Renfrews.

Margaret knew that, it having been pointed out by almost all of her new neighbors and acquaintances. What she hadn't known was that the international star was called 'Julie' by Will Ehrendorf. How odd. She remembered he'd said a long time ago that he knew who she was.

"And I need a neighborly favor tonight," Julia said. "May I get a ride home with you, Will?" She leaned close. "I'll ride in the trunk if I have to. Please, Will? Is Joanne here with you?"

"No," he said. "How did you get here?"

"Dr. Anderson was kind enough to pick me up."

At that, Susanna and Margaret nodded in unison, and Susanna mouthed a stretched-out "boring."

Julia grinned and mimed back, "Exactly."

"Yeah, okay, I guess," Will said. "If you don't mind the grocery van."

"She'd prefer the van, right?" Susanna said. Julia nodded

"When?" asked Will.

"Half an hour. I'll go say my farewells, and then I'll come find you. Alex can organize everyone else."

Julia Levan swept past her son with a smile. She saw Stephanie behind him and stopped and pulled the young woman back into the circle. "Oh, and tomorrow night, please come to dinner, all of you."

"Aunt Julie, we can't," Stephanie said. "You know it's Dad's birthday. I'm making a cake."

"I know that, sweetie," Julia said. "You bring his cake, and all of you, please do come. Six-thirty for drinks. I'll see you then."

Julia left again, allowing herself to be caught briefly by the girls of the outer ring, then moving smoothly back to the end of the room. Like a skilled politician, Margaret thought. But that was part of what it took.

"You could drive your mother home," Will pointed out to Alex.

"Not when she's in full diva mode," Alex said. "OK, who do I have to organize?"

Stephanie rolled her eyes.

Forty-five minutes later, Margaret and Henry and Susanna stood in the dark night on damp grass, watching the one working tail light on the grocery van grow small. Stephanie joined them.

"Holy shit," Susanna said.

"Oh, Susanna," Margaret sighed.

"Holy shit is right," Henry said, to Margaret's surprise. "Good thing nobody stuck a hand between 'em. Could have been electrocuted." It wasn't like Henry to be that observant.

"You think?" Stephanie asked in amazement. "Aunt Julie, my dad?"

"That was so smooth," Susanna said, "the way she cut him out like that. You know what, Margaret? You were right."

"About what? I had no idea."

"He's a heartbreaker, our country friend."

121

♫

Will opened the passenger door of the grocery van. She handed him her violin and gathered her skirt to climb in. She found the seat belt and clicked it together. "Thank you," she said. He gave her back the Strad in its case, and she rested it on her lap.

They rode in silence, the headlights pushing ahead. She didn't know where to begin. Words didn't come.

After a while, Will said, "I never told you how sorry I was about Cathy."

"Your mother wrote mine an awfully nice note. You didn't come to the funeral," she said.

"I went to visit Sharon's grave. She killed him, you know. She grabbed the wheel. I guess it was all she could think of to do."

There it was.

"He was...molesting her?"

"She had the guts that I didn't have."

"Or desperation. I could have called the police. I didn't."

"Could have? You?"

"One night in the park. I got away. I ran away. I never thought about anyone else but myself."

"When was that?"

"The end of the summer before he was killed. Your birthday. You were eighteen."

"The day we..."

"I went down to the park to think about that."

"And then my dad made up your mind."

"Yes," she said, "he did. And then you cheated on me."

"With Chris? You cared?"

She saw the white sign that marked the drive to Greenlea.

"Yeah," he said. "I guess I let myself. It wasn't what I meant to do."

The van struggled up the rutted dirt road. He pulled to a stop at the house and switched off the engine.

Moths fluttered in the headlight beams.

"What's the matter with Stephanie?" Julie asked.

"What? Nothing. What are you talking about?"

"She told me about the DNA. Neither you nor Chris wanted it done. She's wondering if something's wrong. With her," Julie said.

"Nothing's the matter with Stephanie. Chris said no. If Chris changes her mind, I'll change mine."

Julie cranked the van's window down a crack. The sound of bullfrogs rose from the creek that ran down to the lake.

"You're protecting Chris. Does it really need to be secret now?"

His thumbs rubbed against the steering wheel. "That's not for me to say."

"Twenty years."

"Yes," he said.

She reached out and grasped his arm.

"Will," she said, "I take it back. You have permission

to climb our hill. If anyone asks, I said it's okay."

"You mean tomorrow." It wasn't a question.

"I mean tomorrow. Early. At noon."

"Julie, I don't know."

"I don't either, Will. There's so far to go, to meet in the middle. We'll never know if we don't try."

There was silence. She could hear him pull in a breath.

"Your friend, Tina. What about her?"

"Tina's out in L.A. with the latest prospect for Mr. Right."

"Then you're not?" He didn't finish the question.

"Not that we've noticed. She's my best friend. Other people can think what they want. We call it pest control."

A sweep of headlights passed across the trees behind them.

"Tomorrow," he said.

She opened her door and slid to the ground. "If you want to, Will."

♪

"Mom?" Aubrey said, turning from the front seat where her husband was driving. "We're all invited to your friend Julia's house tomorrow night?"

"Apparently so," Margaret replied. "These children are sleepy." Kendra was leaning against her shoulder.

124

Paul had his head in her lap. Susanna was squeezed against the door.

Margaret replayed the look on Kenneth Anderson's face when Susanna told him of Margaret and Henry's invitation to Ms. Levan's home. She knew it was wrong to have enjoyed that moment so much. It was wrong, but so what? In the dark, her face broke into a smile. Tough shit, Margaret thought.

"Alex says," Susanna reported from her corner, "they've been arguing about the invitation to Greenlea for years. Since Steph and her mom went to live with them. Ms. Levan and Stephanie's dad have the same birthday." Henry was driving Alex and Stephanie home. "So, all of a sudden, it's done. He doesn't get it, Alex doesn't," Susanna said.

"Well, I do," said Aubrey.

"Me too," her husband said. "He's a lucky stiff, your friend, Will."

"Richard!" Aubrey said.

"So to speak," Richard added.

125

# CHAPTER TWELVE

### Tomorrow

It had rained. The leaves on the ground were slippery. She'd been under the trees, and he saw she'd thrown the hood of her jacket back. Now she reached the top and saw him standing at the edge of the woods. She came straight to him and reached up to pull his face down to be kissed. His arms held her tight. It felt good, so good, after all these years. She rested her head on his shoulder.

He said, "Julie, what is it you want?"

She pulled away and looked into his troubled eyes. "I want you to be here, Will, waiting for me. I want to give it an honest try."

"You think?"

"I don't know. It's a second chance. We won't know if we don't ever try."

"Ah, Julie." He pulled her into his arms again, and they stood in the afternoon rain till the shudders in his body stopped.

She pulled away. His eyes were bright. The rain had started up again.

"What do you want, Will?" she asked.

"You, Julie." Now he was kissing her again, and holding her tight. She twisted out of his arms, laughing at him.

"Not up here. Not in the rain." She pulled against his hand. "Come on," she said.

He let go and she turned and started down the hill. She was almost running.

He heard himself say "Damn!" Rocks were bouncing down the hill from under his feet. He was trying to see where she was going, trying not to break his neck.

She waited, calling back, "Come on!" Then she took off again.

Damn, he thought, and that was maybe all he thought clearly until much later, at the end of the afternoon. The rain had stopped and the sun had come out. He lay on Julie's bed, holding her, seeing tangerine light that fell on the wall, on the dulcimer resting there on a stand.

He smiled. A long and winding road had come to an end. And a beginning.

⌘

# mle nevin

## Champlain Stories

∞

Changing Course
Ever After
Dulcimer Hill
*FIRE*

Thank you for reading *Dulcimer Hill*. Please visit your favorite book-finding site and leave a brief review. Your feedback is important to me and will help other readers too.

If you'd like to get notifications of new releases and special offers on my books, please join my email list at mlenevin.com.

*mle nevin*
lives and works in Detroit under another name